Feeding the Two-Backed Beast

Erotic short stories by
S.A. Harper

Word Oyster Press

For other work published by
Word Oyster Press
please visit
wordoyster.com

You may contact the writer at:
saharper@wordoyster.com

Cover image © Gresei / Bigstock

ISBN-13: 978-0-9977084-2-4

"In the vigour of his age, he married Gargamelle, daughter to the King of the Parpaillons, a jolly pug and well-mouthed wench. These two did oftentimes do the two-backed beast together, joyfully rubbing and frotting their bacon 'gainst one another."

Rabelais
Gargantua and Pantagruel

Mmm! Bacon.

Simply put, I dedicate this collection to the people — both online and in real life — who inspired these stories. These are your fantasies as much as mine.

Thank you!

Contents

The Adventures of Maggie the MILF and Cereal Boy

There's nothing but sand as far as the eye can see.

OK, this isn't literally sand. It's more like beige lino-leum, punctuated by occasional outcrops of unpacked boxes of canned goods and little old women with blue hair whirring along in their mobility scooters. But, the metaphorical point is, this supermarket — perhaps every supermarket — is a sexual desert on weekday mornings.

And here he is, pushing a cart down the juice aisle, with no oasis in sight. Three aisles down and he cannot find a single distraction to lighten the drudgery of grocery shopping. It's not as if he doesn't have an open mind and an active imagination, but there isn't much to work with. Most people are at work this time of day and won't show up here until late afternoon or early evening. Without a decent salad bar, this store doesn't even have much of a lunchtime crowd.

Not that it's entirely empty. The Coca-Cola delivery man is restocking shelves in the soda aisle and there's Wally, the middle-aged produce clerk, spraying his greens. The cashiers are discussing "The Bachelorette" and their weekend plans. The only customers other than him seem to be the two dozen old folks who arrived in vans from the nearby retirement community just as he pulled into the parking lot.

"That's going to slow me down," he thought, ducking into the Starbucks in order to give them all a good head start. But the grocery carts don't have cup holders, so he only got a small coffee, which the sleepy barista had the good graces to not repeat back to him as "Tall." Ten minutes later and with a slight caffeine rush, he was able to dodge the first three seniors at the deli counter without breaking stride.

But now he's stalled in the cereal aisle. He took too long choosing a box of granola bars and now a little old man is parked in the middle of the aisle, reading the ingredients on a box of Shredded Wheat. Or he would be reading them if he could find his glasses, which are currently on top of his head. He's not in enough of a hurry to ask the old man to let me get by or to turn his cart around. He'll wait.

Killing time, he starts to scan the shelves for the latest varieties of Cap'n Crunch. Then he does the mental math to figure out how many months until September and the temporary, Halloween season return of Count Chocula and Franken Berry. He worries for a moment that he knows that.

Into this unfulfilling reverie falls inspiration in the form of a child's pacifier. It lands at his feet as if it's been spit out by Tony the Tiger himself. He looks around to find a young woman and a grocery cart four or five feet away from him. Sitting in that part of the shopping cart where his produce usually rests, is a happy, babbling child. The little girl is around one, towheaded, and giggling in self-satisfaction at making her mother stop the cart by tossing her pacifier. He has to admire the arm on that girl. Well thrown.

He's slow to look up at the girl's mother. Too slow, he admits in retrospect. The mother is in her late twenties, early thirties — no more than five years older than he is, he's thinking — but seems younger in her white tank top, denim skort, and sandals. Her light brown hair is pulled back in a white scrunchie. He wonders if the diamond stud earrings are real. Who would wear real diamond earrings to the supermarket? He wonders if her breasts are real. Those are remarkable breasts. Her legs are nice, too. He should pick up the pacifier.

"Five second rule?" he asks, smiling, as he starts to hand her the hot pink binky.

The hand that reaches out for the pacifier has a wedding ring and an engagement ring with a pretty serious rock. She sees him see the rings and quickly turns her hand over, opening her palm. He gently places the pacifier in her hand. As she closes her fingers, they brush against his hand. He looks up into her eyes. They remind him of the color of honeydew melons.

"Well, that and a good washing," she says, smiling back at him and rubbing her little girl's legs which are swinging out the back of the cart. "For now, though..." The young woman sticks the pacifier into her own mouth, sucks on it a bit, pops it out, and hands it back to her daughter. "That should work." She looks at him again and laughs a little. "Can't be too careful."

She steps away from the cart. He watches her walk slowly back and forth, looking at the variety of cereal boxes. Her ass is nice, too. She looks at him, probably noticing where he was looking.

"What do you think?" she asks him.

"About what?"

"Cereal, silly. Lucky Charms or Cheerios?"

"You're asking me?"

"Sure. You seemed to be checking out the stock pretty carefully just now. Sydney and I trust you. Which cereal do you think we should buy today? Lucky Charms or Cheerios?"

"Well, Cheerios *are* a classic. A little high in sodium, but much lower in sugar than Lucky Charms. But babies and Cheerios are kinda predictable. And you two seem more like trend setters, more cutting edge. So I'm thinking the Lucky Charms may be better for you. For one thing, they're magically delicious. Two, they have Lucky the Leprechaun. And three? This month, they seem to have these blue moon and red balloon marshmallow shapes that should be really easy to spot when Sydney drops them on your kitchen floor." He grins and hands her a box of Lucky Charms.

"Thank you," she says as she takes the box. "You're very well-informed about cereal. Do you hang out here all day, memorizing packaging and nutrition labels?"

"Actually, I'm more of a bread fondler. You know, like buns? Grinder rolls? But the store manager limits my time in his bread aisle and I've already hit my quota today." He nods and scrunches his face. He wants to keep her talking and doesn't know how. "New delivery of dinner rolls."

"Aren't dinner rolls a little small for fondling?"

"Two in each hand." He raises his eyebrows as if to say, "Everyone knows that."

"Yeah, I can see why store management might want to keep an eye on you." She laughs and puts the box of Lucky Charms in her cart. Sydney has been leaning sideways, looking at the store lights overhead from a different

4

angle. Her mother tickles her, getting her to sit up again.

"Well…" she says, biting her lip just a bit, then smiling again. "We cutting edge gals have to get moving. Places to go. All way too cool to describe." She takes hold of the cart handle and starts to roll away.

"You two take care," he calls after her. "Watch those flying binkies."

She stops and looks back at him over her shoulder. "Why don't cereal boxes have free prizes any more, do you think?"

"Safety issues, " he answers. "Lawyers. Excessive marketing to children. Gotta be one of those."

"OK, so forget the kid cereal. I buy the cereal for my entire family. Her cereal and my cereal. They could just put prizes in my cereal if they're so worried. The cereal for grown ups. Right? Completely different demographic." She pauses. "You can't tell me women wouldn't go for a box of Special K with a free bullet vibe." She laughs and turns back around. With a little over shoulder wave, she, Sydney, and the cart all vanish around the end of the aisle.

Whoa.

How much of this — the stuff that came before — is fact? How much is part and parcel of the possible fantasy that follows? He can't tell or he won't tell. But it's safe to say he found inspiration in the flirting that day and suddenly the supermarket has become a place with at least a chance of something happening. Someone just might take a chance today.

Tomorrow morning, he'll be back in this same grocery, needing to buy the same dozen eggs he's forgetting today after their first encounter. Walking quickly through the produce section to the back of the store, he'll be trying to get in and out in as little time as possible. Today, it's ten items or fewer.

And yet, as he walks along the back of the store on his way to Dairy, he won't be able to resist looking up the cereal aisle when he passes. Unexpectedly, there will be Sydney in a cart again, her mom squatting nearby, retrieving a fallen something or other. He'll smile and walk slowly up the aisle toward them. Sydney will see him and make a silly sound. He'll wave to her and make a face. She'll laugh and hide her eyes.

Sydney's mom, still squatting, will look up and have to grab the cart to keep from falling over. Her skirt will be too short for this particular pose and he'll catch clear sight of shaved pussy. And she'll know that. She'll look right at his face to confirm his smile or his blush or both. At that point, caught with his eyes in the cookie jar, he'll decide to err on the side of upskirt confirmation.

"So, answer me something," he'll say. "Are all young mothers so rushed these days that they run out to the Stop & Shop without their underwear?" He won't be able to say "panties" in the cereal aisle. And really, if you haven't tried it, don't judge.

She'll get up, not looking at him, but smiling and touching Sydney's cheek as she stands beside the cart. He won't be sure if she's surprised to see it's him or worse, that she doesn't remember him at all. But then she'll turn and pin him to the Hungry Jack pancake mix with her directness and her pale green eyes.

"They do," she'll say, "if their husbands won't fuck something they've seen a head come out of."

Not much will be said as they both head together to the same checkout line. He'll have his eggs; she'll have a few items she may or may not need. He'll walk her to her mini-van and stand by the door as she puts her daughter into her car seat.

"Look, this is what this is," she'll say, looking him in the eyes. "It's serendipity. Tomorrow I'm moving to Sharon and I'll be shopping at Roche Brothers from now on. But today, you're here and I'm here. I've got two condoms and Sydney's got a bottle and a "Backyardigans" DVD that will keep her looking the other way for close to an hour." She'll trace a forefinger down his chest and smile. "Carpe diem, Cereal Boy."

"Are you sure?" he'll ask her. That night, he'll wonder why it is that, even in his fantasies, he always looks a gift horse in the mouth. He'll think his fantasies need both a rewind and a rewrite. Perhaps his gift horses need their jaws wired shut.

She'll move closer to him, her shirt touching his belt, her face inches away from his face, looking up. He'll realize again just how much he loves her eyes. "Look. Yesterday, it was you I was flirting with. Today, it could have been someone else, right? But it wasn't. It was you again. What are the chances that we would show up at the same time as each other again? That's fate, right?"

Of course she'll be right. It's suburban kismet.

She'll look away for a second. And when she looks back at him, he'll see her eyes have softened, as if saying "Please?" But that's not what she'll say. Not out loud. Instead, she'll go all Karla DeVito versus Meat Loaf.

"I'm sure. What's it gonna be, boy? Yes or no?"

The wayback of a Dodge Grand Caravan is not the same size as a king, queen, full, or even twin size bed. It's cramped even on the diagonal. But, given that, the windows are tinted so any passersby at the edge of the parking lot won't see anything inside. And, not only does the DVD player fold down from the cab ceiling, it also comes equipped with wireless headphones. Sydney won't hear a thing except for those singing, dancing, colorful animal-like characters with their multi-cultural names teaching important life lessons about pirating and neatness.

He will help her fold down the stowable third row seats and spread a beach towel on the carpeted floor-board. And while this young woman checks on Sydney one last time and locks the doors, he'll remove his sneakers and shorts. There's so much about this situation that should make him too nervous to be excited, and yet his cock will be making a tent out of his boxers just the same.

It's not a mercy fuck, unless she's the one having mercy on him. That'll become even more obvious when she returns to where he is, kicks off her sandals, and they start to kiss. Oddly, her skirt will never come off, even though he'll take off her tank top and bra almost as soon as they start. And his shirt will stay on, even though his boxers won't. He won't know why. Completely naked would be reckless of them, perhaps?

There's something inevitable about a desire that's been given permission to exist in the world. It's a roller coaster going over the crest of that first big hill. Once you've gone as far as the top, all you can do from then on is throw your arms back and scream. What's going to happen is going to happen.

So perhaps even foreplay is excessive in that situation. They'll be beyond foreplay within the first two minutes. Their tongues will be playing tag while he kneads her breasts and she clutches his ass. His cock will nestle between her legs under its own volition, seeking and finding her wet center like some sort of instinct-driven dowsing rod. She'll grab his cock with one hand and slide the head along her slick labia until her fingers drip. Yes, they'll be beyond foreplay.

"Fuck me," she'll say. And she'll say it in such a way that it will be a command, a request, and the granting of permission all at the same time. And with no other words, she'll hand him one of the condoms, flip around, kneel with her bare ass facing him, and bend over, head down on the towel on the van floor.

He'll rip open the condom wrapper and unroll the condom onto his bobbing cock. Her skirt will be half-covering her ass, so he'll flip the cloth up onto her back to expose the whole megillah. Sadly, there won't be enough room in the van for him to back up and enjoy the view. He will want to commit her ass to memory, but he'll also know he's not supposed to.

Maybe he'll be tempted to make this into something more. Maybe he'll start to think he should show off a little, perhaps rub his cock back and forth along her slit, knock on her clit a little with his cock, start to slip inside her but then not.

But she won't be having any of that unnecessary exposition. She'll arch her back and push her ass back into him, reminding him of the insistence at the center of that "Fuck me." She'll turn her head to one side and place it on the mini-van floor to help take her weight. Then she'll reach back with both hands and spread her ass until her pussy is gaping at him, impatient and accusing. So, what else should he do? He'll slip his cock inside her in one short — then one long — deliberate stroke.

And it will be a hard, sweaty fuck. Neither of them will be going for gentle. He'll grab her by the waist and yank her back into him as he thrusts his cock as hard and deep inside of her as he can. Sometimes she'll reach back and grab one of his wrists. Or she'll take one of her hands and push against the inside wall of the van, forcing herself back against him. He won't know if the van is rocking, but each stroke will include a slam of skin on skin, the jolt of his hips striking her ass, all accompanied by her soft, hissing commentary. "Yeah... right there. Harder! Oh, fuck. Fuck, fuck, fuck..."

And somehow... somehow they'll keep going. In and out, body slamming into body, his balls and her breasts swaying, her hand pressing back between her legs, fingers finding her clit. He'll stay hard and she'll stay wet. And neither of them will want to come until they can't help but drop from exhaustion.

Afterward, he'll find himself staring up at the roof of the van, pondering suburbia. She'll toss him a diaper wipe for the used condom and pop her head up over the seat to check on Sydney.

"She's fine," she'll say. "Happy as can be." Turning back toward him, he'll see that her face and chest are flushed, but that somehow she still looks lovely.

"Her husband must be a fucking asshole," he'll think, as if he knows anything. He doesn't know anything. He'll smile. She'll smile back and crawl back over to him.

Kneeling at his side with her palms on his chest, she'll say, "The DVD is only about half over. So... we can go again if you think you can." Laughing, she'll throw a leg over him, straddle his lower legs, grab his cock, and start licking it before he'll have a chance to answer.

"Yeah," he'll softly say. "I think I can manage." By then, that will be obvious, of course. His cock will have never quite gone down all the way. But, as she licks it and plays with his balls, his erection will come back with a hard certainty and leaky enthusiasm. He'll run his fingers through her hair as she runs her tongue along a visible vein before taking his cock into her mouth and throat, bobbing twice, and then letting the head pop out of her tightened lips, making a sound like a distant, wet champagne cork. She'll repeat the move for good measure, watching him lick his lips.

Squatting above his legs, one hand still grasping his erection, she'll lean over and grab the second condom. Ripping open the wrapper with her teeth, she'll take the condom out, roll it onto his shaft, and lower herself onto him. She'll be just as warm and tight as before just, this time, more familiar.

The second time will be a luscious, unexpected anachronism. With their time running out, with all of their knowledge of how temporary and precious that last 20 minutes of DVD will be, one would think that they would be frantic in their motions, that they would fuck like crazed mechanical monkeys on oversized batteries and Red Bull.

But that's wrong. It won't be like that at all. Instead of hurried animal thrashing, this time the sex will be slow and languorous. It will be in the moment. It will be fucking with their eyes open, committing everything to memory — the quality of sunlight as it comes through the tinted mini-van windows, the color of the beach towel, her crooked smile and the bounce of her breasts when she slowly moves on top of him. If they hurry, the end will come all that much sooner. If they take their time, perhaps time will return the favor and take longer. Of course, neither of them will actively think any of this. It will just

11

happen, because that's the way it is supposed to happen.

He's not a big one for talking during sex. Not small talk, not dirty talk, not much talking at all, really. Sex noise is good — grunts and moans and exclamations regarding deity — but coherent thought expressed vocally seems intrusive to him and sometimes out-and-out comical. But this time will be different.

As she rides him, rocking her hips, slowly sliding his cock in and out of her pussy, she'll tell him little things about herself, things that have nothing to do with being a mother, nothing to do with being a wife. She'll push down against his chest and stomach with her hands and he will hold her hands in his hands, trying to move with her, listening to what she tells him, looking at her eyes, occasionally reaching up to cup a breast. He will let her talk and she will let him listen.

Her first boyfriend was named Lawrence, not Larry. When they were 14, they went exploring a house under construction near their middle school. She threw her shirt into the sawdust on the floor and let him lick her boobs. Three years later, she lost her virginity to a guy named Sam who didn't go to her high school and who didn't keep in touch once she let him in her pants. Her best friend from high school, Connie, now lives in Japan, teaching everyday English to groups of young Toyota executives on their way to the Camry assembly plants in the States. She misses Connie a lot more than she ever missed Lawrence or Sam.

She was an athlete. She actually went to college on a tennis scholarship. She looked sexy in the white outfits, but the team wasn't all that good and she quit the team in junior year. She met her husband at college that same year. They moved in together before she was ready and got married two years later at a time that was convenient to everyone's schedule. Pregnancy wasn't convenient to anyone's schedule, but it happened all the same.

She loves her little girl; she's sure of that. She's not sure how or what she feels about her husband. What she is sure of is that she's never been spanked or tied up or fucked up the ass and she wonders if she ever will be. She has a gold vibrator that she calls Jesus because he gets her through her days.

"How do I feel, Cereal Boy?"

And he'll know what she means by that question, what she wants to hear from him as an answer. She'll lean forward until her face is near his, her breasts grazing his chest as she continues to move. He'll place his hands on her smooth ass, her curving waist and hips. And he'll tell her how tight her pussy feels wrapped around his cock. He'll describe for her in some detail how he can feel her warmth and her juices through the condom. He'll compare the feeling of her cunt to hot fudge sundaes and to Beethoven's Ninth and this will make her smile.

"Thank you," she'll say, leaning back and placing his hand on her belly. "Make me come."

Is her belly less toned than it was two years ago? How would he know? Are there faint traces of stretch marks? He won't notice. It won't be important. He'll slip his thumb between them and press her clit against his cock as he slides in and out of her. Only then will she close her eyes. And as she gets closer and as she starts to bite her bottom lip, he'll wonder who or what she is thinking about. Then, without warning, she'll open her eyes and look into his. And she won't look away as she comes, allowing only one cry out loud before holding it in, letting go and staying quiet, all at the same time.

"Now you," she'll say, starting to roll her pelvis, slowly riding his cock, enjoying his cock, committing his transitory cock to permanent memory.

She'll be dressed seconds after the DVD starts to roll credits. As he finishes getting his own clothes and shoes back on, she'll already be tickling Sydney and finding her a snack from a backpack on the front passenger seat.

He'll think it best to just let the moment go and walk away with a smile and a wave. Two shopping carts that passed in the night and all that. He'll get out of the van and start to walk away.

But she'll call after him. "Wait a second!" She'll run over to him and hand him the bag with his carton of eggs. "You wouldn't want to forget these, would you?"

"No. I might need to juggle those later." He'll have to joke, because he'll feel sad for some reason, like he's about to experience the loss of something he didn't even know he had.

And that's when she'll rise up on her tiptoes and kiss his cheek as if they were old friends.

"Maggie. My name is Maggie."

He'll smile and start to say something, but she'll already be turning around to go. But, before she does go, she'll wheel around and jab a finger into his chest, look him in the eyes, and say, "Just remember me, Cereal Boy. Think you can do that?"

"Yeah, Maggie. I can do that."

Rigid Crystal Lattice

Almost... almost... there!

A drop of water falls from the ice cube I am holding above your wrist. The drop hits your skin next to the thin blue veins snaking along the underside, crossing the tendons. The drop hesitates, then rolls off the side, under your wrist and maybe down your forearm a little before it's lost in the darkness of the sheets. I'm using my fingers to melt the ice and it's predictably making my entire hand cold. You're wet. I'm wet. Even in your present position, you can appreciate the symmetry in that.

Another drop falls, this one just missing the black cuff velcroed around your wrist. Your fingers briefly unwrap from around the rope that runs from the cuff to the bedpost, then quickly wrap around it again. You pull lightly and the bedpost creaks. Each of your wrists — each ankle, too — has its own black cuff, each cuff with its own rope tied to its own bedpost.

You agreed to this. You took off all your clothes when I asked. And then you let me lay you down on the bed and spread you wide, tying you to the four corners. I put a pillow beneath your head so that it was propped up enough for you to watch me strip to my black bra and panties.

And when I took off those same panties, you voluntarily opened your mouth and let me stuff them inside.

Yes, you agreed to all of this and more. You even nodded, allowing me to tie your balls to the footboard with a length of twine. You acquiesced to the blindfold I put on you before I left the room and made you wait while I got the ice from the kitchen. Now, after just a little play, your head doesn't even turn toward the falling cold your eyes can't see. You're drifting down, fighting to surface only to let go and sink deeper.

You hold your breath, waiting for the next drop to fall. And when it does fall on your forearm, you inhale sharply through the cloth in your mouth. This drop just sits there on your skin, so I bend over to lick it off. Another drop falls, this time in the inside crease of your elbow. And then another drop falls on your upper arm. I watch that one drip toward your arm pit. That must tickle.

What next? You're probably wondering the same thing. Maybe you think you know. I hold the ice cube in my hand so that it isn't dripping on you at all. Wrapped in my fingers, sitting in my palm, the ice melts more quickly. You are still holding your breath, still waiting for the next single cold drop. Waiting. Waiting.

And when I turn my hand over, my fingers pointing down over your chest, six or seven drops of water rush down my fingers, over the ice cube, and then drop onto your hard, bare nipple. You gasp, back arching. Harder. I think your nipple looks harder, tighter now than it did before. Mine would do that too, I think. I lean over and take your nipple in my mouth, flicking the cool nub back and forth with my tongue. It stays hard, rolling and dodging beneath my tongue. I suck slightly, licking the entire areola now. It doesn't even take my whole tongue. Men's areolas are so small. And really, your nipple is no bigger than a fuse bead.

You're already breathing rapidly when I pull my mouth away. But when I quickly substitute the cold flat surface of the ice cube where my warm tongue had been, you cry out (as best you *can* cry out with a mouth full of satin and lace) and toss from side to side. The ropes won't let you go far, of course. After 30 seconds or so, I take the ice cube away and lower my mouth back onto your cold, wet nipple.

In a way, the warmth soothes you. You stop trying to move, but you still can't get your breathing under control. You have been breathing hard — mostly through your nose, but also through and around the wadded ball of cloth in your mouth. Your breathing isn't slowing down, which is good since I don't want it to. I want to keep you excited and guessing. What I want counts. Gently, I clench the hard bead of your nipple between my front teeth and flick the tiny part that sticks into my mouth with my tongue.

The thing is, you've had me tied up like this several times before. I've been blindfolded and spread-eagled on this same bed… sometimes on my back, sometimes on my belly. There have been gags and plugs, nipple clamps and glass dildos shaped like tentacles. I've been tickled and spanked. I've had a Hitachi wand tied to my leg with the head pressed against my cunt and I've watched you turn it on and walk away. And each time, I've had orgasm after orgasm, leading to tears, but always ending up in your arms. I've learned how to play. You taught me.

I know you would lick your lips, if you could. I bring the ice to your mouth and rub it across your lips, first the top and then the bottom. I let the ice linger on your bottom lip so that some water accumulates in your mouth. You can use that. And besides, we're not done.

Standing up, I place the first piece of ice in my mouth and take another larger cube from the dish on the bed stand. I hold this new, larger piece of ice in my hand, grasping it in my upturned fist, feeling the cold water dripping down the back of my hand. I look at you. I can see that you are wondering what's going to happen next. You want to hold your breath in anticipation, but can't. The more you try, the more confused and ragged your breathing gets. You are trying to listen for clues, but I'm not giving any. One minute. Two minutes. I stand there for three minutes without making a sound. Then I lean over and softly whisper in your ear... "Don't worry. There's more."

I get on the bed, kneeling beside your waist. Briefly, I consider carefully positioning myself between your legs, straddling the string that runs from your slightly purple balls to the footboard. I've left a little slack; you can move a little on the bed without tugging too much. I weigh whether or not I can throw a leg across your chest, position my feet on your arms, and put my pussy as close to your face, your nose, your mouth with the soaked black panties sticking out. But again, I don't want to undo the string on your balls and I don't want to risk moving you too much accidentally. I'm a considerate Domme.

I place one flat surface of the ice cube on your sternum and slowly slide it down your chest. Drops slide down your ribs to either side at random. The ice starts to encounter hair a couple of inches above your bellybutton. That slows the water down somewhat. But by the time I have slithered the ice that extra two inches, your belly-button has filled with cold meltwater and is spilling over and down the side of your belly onto the bed. I lean over and suck the puddle from the depression.

The most interesting thing to me about having your balls tied to the footboard is the effect it has on your erection. Normally, if you had a boner and you were on your back like this, your cock would be hard, but mostly down, pointing toward your head, and hovering above your belly. Sure, if I touched it or if you tensed your muscles, it would pop up closer to vertical. But mainly, it would be down. But with your balls and all that scrotum skin being pulled toward your feet, your erection is standing straight up. It moves a bit this way and that, but it doesn't have the slack to fall toward your stomach.

I decide to park the ice cube in your pubes. Doing that frees the hand that was holding the ice cube to run cold fingers over the hot, tight skin on your balls. You probably shaved them last week; there's hair — a bit longer than stubble — pricking at my fingers. The skin is pulled tight by the string looping around the base of your sack. I threaded the string through the loops at the top, between your balls and ran that to the footboard. Your balls are distinct — two eggs in a shiny basket o'skin. They can't do anything when I touch or tap them with my cold fingers. Your cock, on the other hand, jumps and twitches back and forth.

The ice in my mouth has already melted, so I lean forward and replace it with the cube I left on you. I open my mouth, envelop the ice, partly close my mouth, and suck the cool meltwater from your pubes. It makes a terrific, sensual sound. I hear the bedframe creak as you pull against the ropes. Feeling frustrated, are you?

I move the ice around in my mouth until my tongue, my cheeks, my lips feel cold and numb. The ice slips to one side of my mouth — inside my right cheek. It's as good a place as any to hold it, for now. I stick out my cold, cold tongue and lick up the length of your warm, twitchy cock. You quickly move your hips, but just as quickly stop, reminded the hard way that your don't have a lot of room to move. The string running from your balls to the footboard is naggingly taught. Not that I can tell whether your instinct is to move toward or away from my tongue. It doesn't matter since either way is more than your balls can take. For fun, I reach out and pluck the string as if I'm playing a harp.

The other interesting thing about having your balls tied to the end of the bed is that it doesn't leave any extra skin on your cock for my hand to slide up and down the shaft. You're circumcised; maybe that's part of it. But now that I take your cock in my hand and dribble cold water on it from my mouth, I can feel that the skin won't move. This blowjob will have to be all mouth, no hand. And as I wrap my lips around the head and let it slip inside my icy mouth, I decide that will be just fine.

Cold, isn't it? If you could cry out, you would. Instead, your head lifts off the pillow and you gasp through your nose and through the cloth in your mouth. You moan what sounds like protest. I assume that's more the anticipated cold, not from pain. Your legs, tied by the ankle to the bedposts, bend and move in spasms from side to side. Your back arches and your fingers pull hard on the ropes binding your arms. I bob my head, taking your warm cock deep into my mouth. The remaining ice cube finds the head, the side of your cock. Cool water slips past my lips and dribbles down your shaft and runs between your legs onto the bed. Soon the ice cube is gone and my mouth is as hot as your cock.

I tighten my lips, bob faster, and take you deeper. Five bobs, then tight suction so that the head of your cock pops out of my lips when I pull up. I repeat the process. Eight bobs this time… and pop. And again. Ten bobs and an emphatic pop.

We've been together long enough now that we know each other's orgasm tells. What we say, how we breathe, the way our fingers clutch or our toes point, the taste of my pussy or your precum, how swollen our bits and bobs are just before we cum. And even though you're tied up and gagged, I'm pretty certain that I'll be able to tell when you're about to have an orgasm. Not quite yet. Almost. Five bobs and pop. Closer. I can feel the head of your cock getting bigger. Four bobs and… no pop.

I sit up and watch. Your cock flutters as your stomach muscles tighten and release. Close, but not quite. Try again. Five bobs, pop. Just about there. Three bobs and…

Again, I immediately open my mouth and sit up to watch. I got it just right. You start to ejaculate, but only the beginning of that first, starter spurt comes out. If I were to touch your balls, tap your shaft, run a tongue over the head of your cock right now, you would cum, just like that. But that's not what I'm going to do. I'm not touching you at all. I'm waiting for your orgasm to recede. Waiting, but not waiting too long. I touch your cock with my finger to test. It seems safe enough. You moan something that could either be a complaint or a plea.

I bend down and lick the cum from the head of your cock. And then I take you into my mouth again. Four bobs and pop. Six bobs and pop. It won't be as long this time. Four bobs and pop. So close… Two bobs and…

I open my mouth and sit up. One more bob would have been enough. One touch now would be enough. But

I'm not touching you. There's no orgasm. Just thick, milky white cum pouring from your cock. You aren't spurting; you're spilling what you can't keep inside any more. The cum oozes down the side of your cock and pools in your pubic hair. You moan, breathing hard and thrashing your head back and forth on the pillow. Ejaculation without orgasm. I consider this a success.

I reach across your chest and take off your blindfold. Your eyes are shiny. You aren't the type to cry, but I can tell you're in an interesting space right now. I wonder what the first thing you would say to me if I were to take the gag out of your mouth. Not that I do. Not that I'm untying you either. Instead, I walk over to the dresser and take my cellphone out of my bag. You watch me, eyes wide in piss and disbelief, as I call my best friend.

"Hey. Yeah. No, nothing much. Just hanging out with Sam. How 'bout you? Really? When did this all happen?"

As I talk, I sit back down on the side of the bed. Casually, I spread the cum around on your stomach. Each drop expands to the size of a silver dollar. I have to scrape most of it out of your pubes, since you didn't so much spurt as dribble when you came. But when I'm done, your entire belly is glistening. I move the phone away from my mouth, lean close to you, and blow across your belly. I bet that feels colder than all the ice. You look at me. It's a look that combines anger, surrender, and frustration. I smile, put the phone back to my face, and get up off the bed.

"No! You've got to be kidding. That sucks. Are you going to do something about it?"

I give you a wink and a little wave, turn, and walk out the bedroom door.

22

Distraction

Hey, Ms. Muse. How's Monday morning in the Lone Star state?

Dreary. I'm too bored to be horny. Fix me.

You're there. I'm here. All I need to do is write you wetter there or imagine you here. If I do the latter, will that work on the former?

I don't know. Try me.

My home office has three desks arranged in a loose, squared-off U. So I'm typing now at the computer on the desk in the middle — the bottom of the U — with desks to my right and to my left. The left desk is covered with reference books and half-filled notepads, all related to the project I'm working on this week. The right desk has the laptop and two stacks of loose papers. There's a window behind the right desk. If I look over my right shoulder and over that desk, I can see the street. Nothing is happening in the street. Nothing is happening in my home office, if you don't count my work. And you probably wouldn't count my work, if you were here.

Are you going to work all day? How long are you going to make me wait?

That's just it. If you were here, I'd have a narrow window for writing. If I get up early, maybe I could get in half a day before you came to find me. I won't stop typing as you enter the room, walk up behind me, and run your fingers across my shoulders. No reaction. You can wait.

But will you wait? I imagine you move aside the laptop and papers on the desk to my right. Saying nothing, you turn your back to me so that you face the desk, and you bring one knee up onto the desktop. The desk creaks as you pull yourself up and place the other knee on the desk. You kneel on the desk, your ass towards me and your head towards the window. I don't look. I keep typing, taking it all in out of the corner of my eye. Then you reach back and slowly inch your skirt up, inch by inch.

Which panties are you wearing today? How long do I make you wait before I turn in my chair and take those panties down? And then... do I go back to my work, do you think? Or do I leave you there, a pretty display within arm's reach? A delicious distraction, but I can't quite picture it yet. Any ideas?

> *I flip my short purple skirt up onto my back so you can see the wet spot growing in my gray boyshort panties.*
>
> *I grow tired of you not diving into me, so I look back at you with wide eyes and a whimper.*
>
> *You're still trying to look like you're ignoring me, but you've almost stopped typing.*
>
> *I see you sneak a look at my ass and I know I have you. Serves you right. You should have paid attention right away.*
>
> *I slide my fingers inside my panties and bite my bottom lip. I'm sure you see how the fabric moves with every stroke of my fingers...*

I stop typing. I don't have my usual "writing music" playing today and so, without the sound of my fingers on the keyboard, the only sounds I can hear are me shifting uncomfortably in my seat, the creak of the desk you're on, and a faint sticky clicking sound of your fingers moving in your panties. I try to appear disinterested, but realize my cock isn't being stoic. I turn my chair to look.

You've stopped whimpering. You know I'm looking now. You knew it when I stopped typing. You knew it before I slowly spun around in my chair. And now? Now you know I'm watching, just beyond arm's length. You know you can put on a show.

You straighten your back, rising back up onto your knees. You had been leaning forward, supporting yourself with your left arm while your right hand did its business. I can see how wet that right hand is now as you reach both hands to your sides and shimmy your panties down off your ass and halfway to your knees. Your Manic Panic red hair falls across your face as you look over your shoulder and smile at me before dropping back down to your former position — left arm propping you up as the fingers of your right hand slip back between your legs.

I wheel my chair nearer, near enough that my face is less than a foot away. Your fingers move more deliberately. The forefinger and ring finger spread your labia apart while your middle finger disappears and reappears in the center. I love the colors of your pussy, the way they change as the bits and bobs heat and swell. I lean closer still, close enough that you can extend your hand and tickle my chin with wet fingers, close enough that I wonder whether your pussy feels the sigh that leaves my lips.

Soaked. Literally soaked. My panties are a darker shade of gray now.

25

I don't want to leave you hanging, but I'm going to my classes now. Duty calls.

But you should send me more of this for when I get out. I'm kinda greedy and majorly cum hungry. ;)

I run my hand up and down the outside of your right thigh as I think about where this should go. You have gone out of your way to interrupt me. I could punish you. There are rulers in the jar on the edge of the desk. I could use one of those to smack your ass until it's pink and red. I could humiliate. There are Sharpies in the desk drawer. I could draw on your skin — arrows pointing to your openings, words like "wet" and "wants it." Or I could turn on my webcam, point it at you there on the other desk, fill my screen with your ass, your juicy pussy, your panties around your knees. Or… or I could do what I do.

I take off my glasses, turn in my chair, and lean back, placing my glasses aside and next to my keyboard. Then I spin back around to you. I lean in again, brushing my cheek (which may be a bit bristly… when did I shave?) along your tender, inner thigh. I breathe in the smell of you… the fresh-washed soap smell of your thighs giving way to the damp smell of your pussy. Up close, I see how the pink and brown lips swell and glisten. It looks like an oyster and it smells like you.

I lean closer. I brush my nose against your labia and you gasp, arching your back a bit, trying to push into the touch… any touch. I slide the bridge of my nose between your lips, avoiding your clit, starting just above it and sliding between your labia and then out. I do this again and again until my nose is wet and your pussy unfurls. There are so many ways for this to go, I think, as I burrow my nose deeper into you and stick out my tongue.

Classes? Classes??? How can you go to classes at a time like this?

> *I AM still working on my degree. I also work 15 hours a week at the school. I went to my two morning classes and now I'm in my office at work... luckily alone since these texts and story parts you're sending me are driving me INSANE. I've soaked through my slacks.*

> *I would give anything to slide my hand down my pants and panties and feel how wet I am with my fingers... but someone might come into the office. Squirm squirm.*

> *What would you like? You've sold me. I'm hooked.*

Of course, that IS one big advantage of working from home. If I want to get off in the middle of the day, I can. <pause> And I did. Yet MORE time away from my chapter, thank you very much. LOL

Where were we? I suspect your knees are getting a bit sore from kneeling on my desk all afternoon. And it looks like I left my tongue hanging out, too. That could be awkward. And probably dry.

Good question. What WOULD I like?

> *I think you would LOVE to dive in and taste me. I'm sweet.*

> *And I would love to just lay back and let you... run my fingers through your hair (with the most attention being paid to your graying temples, which I think are hot).*

> *Would you love to tease me? I would love you to tease me.*

> *I would love to let you take me. 'Fill me...*

What is it you taste like? You're right that you taste sweet, but I can't quite place the taste. It seems more apple than pear, but more pear than peach. Maybe it isn't a fruit at all. Maybe it's marzipan. Maybe marshmallow crème. I feel you contract on my nose and moan lightly. I'll think about it later.

My hand has been on your ass cheek. I slide it side-ways — in and down — until my thumb can replace my nose in your folds. My thumb slips inside you so easily only to have you grab it so hard. I fight your grip and pull my thumb out a bit, so that only part of it is inside you... and you flutter, gripping at my thumb, trying to pull it back inside. Do you do that consciously or does a pussy just know how to do it on its own? I give you back the whole thumb, slipping it inside you as deep as it can go, rotating my hand and rubbing your ass with my out-stretched fingers.

There's liquid rolling down my thumb, my wrist, my forearm. Some of it's me; most of it's you. My tongue can't catch it all. My tongue has been up and down your length, poking and licking and nestling in beside my thumb, trying to make the opening two thumbs wide. I take the nearest labia between my lips and pull.

You have both forearms on the desk now. You clutch the back edge as if the desk is tipping back toward me and you could fall into my face. One minute your head is hanging down; the next minute, you've thrown it back, pointing your face to the window and the bright midday sky lighting up your closed eyes. There's a subtle wiggle of your ass. You tilt it, play with the angle and curve of your back. You fine-tune your position, pushing against me, pulling away, trying anything you can to find-keep-apply my nose, my tongue, my lips, my teeth behind my lips —

anything I have that's wet and warm, soft or hard — to get it in contact with you.

But mostly, you want some part of me to find your clit, say hello, and become its new best friend. You yelp as I flick you with my tongue.

Maybe it is apple.

> *Panting. That was just so... right. I don't understand how you know what I like without knowing me.*
>
> *But at least you didn't know mine's more like peach. ;)*

Dammit. I prefer peach even though I said apple. There's nothing quite like biting into a ripe, juicy peach, trying to keep the juice from rolling down your chin. Yes, your pussy should absolutely be peach.

> *You should know that if someone had their hands on me the way you described, I would be a goner.*
>
> *I wish I knew who you were. :(*

No one knows about you. You're my secret peach.

> *I like being a secret.*

Are you going to help me out with where this story goes next? I could lick you until you cum and fall off the desk, if you want. And I do have ideas. But... maybe I could get a little input from you about now. What next, M?

> *I would love to help with the story, but I can't. This is truly torture. I don't even have the time to sit on here and wait for you and your words, but I do it anyway. I guess that says a lot about how nice your words are...*

I want to taste you. I want to choke on you before I cum. Pretty please?

I was thinking that I knew where this pleasant distraction of yours was going. Once we got started, why would my tongue stop circling your clit? Why would I take my thumb out of you when it could stay there where it is now, stretching you wide? Why would I want to stop breathing in the smell of sex dripping off of my wet hand and sleeve, dripping out of you? Why stop tasting you, drinking you? Why would we stop before you cum?

But it seems I'm wrong. Either you're restless or maybe horny for something more than this quick one-way fix. The desk creaks as you pull away from me, leaving my head behind. My thumb slips out of you and suddenly feels cold in the office air. You slip sideways, off your knees, staying on the desk but now lying on your left side, head at the edge of the desk, facing me with hungry eyes and a flushed face. You open your mouth and wait. I stand up from my chair, unbuckle my belt, unsnap and unzip my jeans, and pull both jeans and boxers down past my erection, letting them fall to the floor.

There's no subtlety to a boner pointing straight out at any person's face. That you're both in that position pretty much says it all. So it shouldn't surprise me that there's no subtlety to your next move. You reach out one hand, grab me by the balls, and pull. You pull and I step forward. You pull and now I'm close enough that the head of my cock is at your lips. You lick the clear liquid from the tip, moan, then pull me closer still. You open your mouth, pull one last time, and I slip the head of my cock inside.

My cock fills your mouth. You look up at me, raise yourself up on your left forearm to get a better angle, and I push ahead another inch…and then another and another. Purposely, you push ahead, not stopping, eyes on mine, taking my cock in until you choke.

I pull part way out and you recover, eyes still watering. But you won't give up. Again, you tug my balls and I slip my cock back inside your mouth and back into your throat. Your grip on my balls urges me to slowly fuck your mouth. I never argue with someone who has my balls.

You're twisted on the desk in a way that means your right leg is bent. I put my left hand under your skirt and slide one finger between your wet folds. You won't stop looking at me. You won't let go of my balls or my cock. You won't give up on having my cock in the back of your throat. I slip two fingers inside of you and pull.

Something's gotta give.

> *More! I want as much of this story as I'm allowed. I want as much as I can get.*
>
> *But you should make me beg a little.*

I wonder if you mean I should make you beg for more story, beg for something special IN the story, or both.

Guess I'll just have to guess.

> *Beg to be pleased.*
>
> *Beg to be fucked.*
>
> *Beg to be filled with you.*
>
> *I want penetration. Graphic penetration.*
>
> *I want you to spread my legs open while I'm sitting on the edge of the desk. I want you to tease me with the head of your cock and make me beg for you to put it in.*
>
> *I want your breath rasping on my neck because you are so close to me as you thrust.*

By the way, I'm soaked again. Changing my panties again. Doing laundry tonight. All because of you.

Something's gotta give. I have two fingers curled inside your pussy. They're drenched and you're squeezing them like a boa that's found a rat. It won't take much for you to cum. I know that. And I won't deny you that. Just not right now. Besides, that's not what you're really wanting anyway, is it?

I reach down with my right hand and take your hand from around my balls. I grip your wrist hard and bring your clenched fist and your arm up tight against the side of your head. Now your head is trapped under your own arm. My cock is still in your warm mouth, but you can't control the motion any more. I slowly fuck your face. I move in and out — slowly — not wanting to actually cum. Not yet. Not here. Right now, I just want my cock to be in your mouth when *you* cum.

And you do cum. You're hooked by fingers fucking you on one end and pinned at the other end with your wrist held tight by my hand and my cock deep in your mouth and throat. You've been breathing through your nose. But when your orgasm hits, you gasp for air, shuddering, crying muffled sounds that are buried in your throat where I can feel them vibrating the head of my cock. The whole desk shakes.

I slip my shining, throbbing, spit-covered cock from your mouth and let you breathe. Your pussy is clenching my fingers, letting go, then clenching again. How long do I give you before I can get you on your feet? Not long. You shouldn't catch your breath. I shouldn't allow you to be without part of me inside you for that long. I slip my fingers out from between your legs, reach behind you, and start to pivot your rear off the desk. Your panties hit the floor before your feet. You're wobbly, but standing. I take you by the arms and turn you away from me and toward the window.

"Take off the skirt, Megan, and lean against the desk."

I loveeeee this part. Best part yet, I'd say.

But you know that. You know what I like now, so what you write is growing more dangerous and closer to home.

Of course, now I'm almost obligated to keep you waiting for the next part. ;)

More more more more more! This whole section is too much. I'm losing it. I AM SO WET!

Seriously, I'll be back late tonight. That'll give you a chance to fold your undies.

Oh please come back sooner. I want more!

When you come back, will you cum inside me?

I don't know. When I get back, I was thinking I should maybe catch up on some reading...

No! Release me. Help me finish, you tease! ;)

I love it.

This is probably one of those times when I should be extorting something, quid pro quo. But I guess I won't.

Maybe. <evil smile>

I'm really not sure what you're complaining about. You already came once.

Zero complaints.

Only begging.

And I think you like that ;)

A bit weak in the knees, you lean against the desk. At first you just rest the tops of your legs against the edge, your hands flat on the wood, your arms straight and head up. You look back at me over one shoulder, as if to ask, "What's next?" Instead, what you say is, "Please?"

I slip my hand between your legs from behind and stroke your cunt again. Your neck bends and your head drops as your lean back, trying to get away from the desk enough for your hips to move. I hold my fingers still and let you ride them, grind and slip-slide on them.

"Please what? Isn't this what you want?"

"I want your cock. In me. Please."

There. You've said it. But having said it doesn't mean your hips have stopped rocking. Saying it out loud doesn't make my hand any less wet or mean you move away when I slip two fingers inside you again. No, you take the fingers, two knuckles deep.

"Lean forward and get down on your arms."

You lower your shoulders, trying not to move your legs or your ass, trying hard not to lose contact with my fingers, still in you. Your upper body is now resting on your forearms. You object quietly when I disengage my fingers from you so that I can move your feet apart and back so that you have to lean more to reach the desk.

"That's better," I say to the back of your head. I trace my fingertips down your spine, between your cheeks, and back between your legs. Still drenched.

For a minute or two, I let you ride the side of my hand. I watch the clouds out the window. Several crows fly from one tree to the next. I watch your shoulders shake. You're trying so hard to move without moving. You rock your pelvis and grind away on my hand. You shift, moving your feet even farther apart. You tip your ass up. I slide my hand from between your legs and push down on your back with wet fingers. You're ready.

I lean over you and kiss your shoulder. You feel my thighs pushing against your ass and my weight on your back. You feel my cock between your legs, tapping up against your pussy. I stand back up and carefully position the head of my cock only slightly between your lips, getting my cock wet, feeling how your pussy tries to grab it. You are already trying to push away from the desk to swallow me up, but you can't. My hand is on your back, pushing you down, keeping you still.

"Please! Please make me cum again!" You say it to the desk, but the sound of it fills the office. It's not begging or pleading. It's not desperation or despair. It's like you're a long arrangement of dominos, waiting for me to topple the first one in line. All that preparation. All that waiting. All that knowledge of what inevitably comes next if I would just tip over that first domino.

I push inside you. I moan. You hiss some variation on "Fuck, yes!" And for one moment, I transcend the action and the movement. I'm lost in the feeling of you wrapped around me, all of your hot wet girl tightness, how it's so juicy and sweet, pulsing with life and potential.

And when that revelry passes? I reach out with one hand, take hold of your hair, and pull.

> I have chills.
>
> That's what I like. I like feeling the buildup. Mine, yours. I love the anticipation of someone cumming. Yummmmmmm.
>
> I want you, and I do not even know you.

I thrust hard into you, pushing you up against the desk. The fingers of my left hand are in your hair, holding

35

it, pulling back so that your head tips back, your neck stretched tight. Your mouth is open, half breathing, half gasping. I can't see your eyes, but I imagine them wide open, staring out the window and up into the trees in disbelief.

My right hand is pushing down on your back. Your back is arched, your ass tipped toward me, pussy spread wide to meet my thrusts. Again and again, my motions are countered by the desk hitting the wall and window sill, by me pulling you back to meet me. I take my right hand off your back and slap your ass hard. You yelp. I slap it again. You whimper.

In a porn movie, this part would last for 15 minutes or more. But that isn't real. This is real. And this reality comes down to a few short minutes of end game: my cock filling and stretching, one end bumping a cervix, the other knocking against a swollen clit.

And then…? Well, everyone knows what happens then. You can tell I'm going to cum and you will yourself to follow. I close my eyes and disappear into the redness of light from the window leaking through my eyelids. I drop like a stone into the feeling of emptying myself into you. My knees shake with the idea of you wanting that, needing that. I quiver so much that it hardly registers that you are doing the same.

I lean over onto you, breathing hard. I touch your cheek. When my shrinking cock slips from you, you spill me onto the office floor like pale ink.

Look what we've written, you and I.

You're brilliant.

I can't wait to fuck someone. If I were there with you and your desks, I'd make you do all of this. Just like you wrote it.

Well, when you fuck someone this week, I hope they appreciate how I've given you incentive and inspiration. :)

Spank me next time?

Of course. Write me tomorrow and tell me about the wooden spoons in your kitchen.

Fuck yeah.

The Orchard

"It's getting late and I promised my wife I'd be home in time for us to go into town for dinner. So, if you kids don't mind, I'm just going to close up and head home." The old man puts the last crate in the back of his pickup truck and closes the gate. The small roadside stand is empty. He doesn't need to put up a "Closed" sign.

"That's OK, sir," I hear you tell him. "We didn't mean to keep you. We just saw your stand and the apple trees and decided to stop."

"No problem. I hate to make you pick your own, but you've got your bag. The sun should stay up for another hour or so. Just walk up this road through the orchard. You should find some nice Cortlands on the trees just over that hill. I wouldn't drive up there, though. The roads are a bit rutted and muddy."

He looks over at me, sitting in the car with my bare legs hanging out of the open passenger side door. "Young lady, do you have some old shoes?" I'm wearing black dress shoes. They're not fancy, but they're fancier than the sneakers you're wearing. They also match the black skirt I'm wearing. Neither exactly screams "Take me apple picking."

"I have a pair of sneakers in the back," I lie, turning on the charm. If it will help move this along, I'm even willing to hike my skirt up a few inches.

I can't believe you let me think we were going for a romantic dinner at some little, picturesque Vermont inn and we ended up here instead. As I was getting dressed earlier, I was picturing us sitting by a fire, each of us with a glass of Cabernet, you looking smokily into my eyes as an attentive, yet easily overlooked waiter, brings us small plates of this and that— probably more than a couple involving local cheeses. I dressed for that dream and you let me do it. Now, here I am, about to sprain my ankle for some apples we could get at a farm stand tomorrow on our way back to Boston.

The old man smiles. "Not sure that skirt is the most practical thing for apple picking. Have her hold the ladder for you." He shoots me and my legs another look. "Or not. I suppose. Your choice." He sighs and gets in the truck. "Have fun. Remember, just down the road and over the first hill. Can't miss it."

"Yes, sir. We've got it. Thanks!"

We watch as the truck pulls away and drives off down the curving, two-lane road. You walk back over to the car and stand in front of me.

"Did you two have a nice chat?" I ask. "A little XY bonding over the harvest?" I look up at you and smile.

"He was a little concerned about you picking apples in that skirt. I assured him that you had every intention of leaving it in the car. That seemed to put his mind at ease." I try to kick you, but you duck out of the way of my foot. "Liability issues, I guess." This time, I laugh. "C'mon, Nicole. Let's get going." You help me out of the car and we set off down the road through the orchard.

The air is turning cool as the sun gets lower in the sky. The light is visibly yellower than it was when we pulled off the road. The shadows are getting longer; they trail yards behind us as we walk. I'm squinting as I pick my way behind you down the dirt road. The orchard spreads over this hill and the next. Beyond the hills, the broad valley tilts up into the mountains, which are rapidly losing light, turning a dusty purple.

Suddenly you turn, cocking your head towards the grove of trees. I freeze, trying to hear what you heard. You point into a low branch of one of the trees labeled "Macoun" and I see a big barred owl sitting there, blinking its round eyes and watching the pile of leaves near the tree's roots. It suddenly swoops and comes up with some poor rodent in its hooked beak. I cringe. You put an arm around my waist.

"That's the thing about nature. Beauty. Gore. It's all there, side-by-side, every minute of every day. What you see…" you kiss my cheek. "…all depends on where you look. So, I suggest you don't look there. Look for apples." You pull me forward, down the road.

I'm not sure I'm reassured by that, even if I give it credit for being more than the bullshit it is, but we continue along the road, your arm around my waist and your hand clutching mine. You're holding me up a bit. The farmer was right. The road is a muddy, rutted mess. You're going to owe me for these shoes, one way or another. They aren't Jimmy Choos, but I still like them.

"What are we doing out here again?"

"We're picking apples. See? We have a bag and everything. The farmer said we should find some nice ones just over this hill." Sure enough, rounding a little curve and popping over the hill, we find the Cortland trees, heavy with fall fruit. We can hear the owl in the distance. I can no longer see the road. There are no signs of houses near-by. It's just us, our bag, the trees, and a ladder.

You hand me the empty bag. The ladder is flat on the ground, parallel to the outermost row of trees. You pick the ladder up and move it so that it slants up into the nearest apple tree. You hop up onto the bottom rung and bounce, demonstrating that the ladder is solid and unlikely to move.

"Up you go!" you say to me, hopping down from the ladder and gesturing as if to say, "Step this way!"

"Me? Why me? This is your idea."

"I have to hold the ladder. And fend off the owls and apple weasels. C'mon. The sooner we finish, the sooner we can go." You pat the ladder and gesture up into the tree. I hand you back the bag and start to climb.

I go up several rungs, just enough so that I can reach the first ripe apples. At first, you stand at the bottom of the ladder, hands bracing both verticals. Your face is level with the backs of my smooth calves. What you see all depends on where you look... and you let your gaze wander up my legs and up my skirt.

You're cruel, making me climb in spite of my vertigo, knowing how dizzy I'll be. And you should know my legs aren't up to this, how achy my muscles are from last night. My breath catches as I try to go up one more rung. I have one foot on the higher rung, one on the rung below. I can't look down this way, but I feel your eyes on me. I swallow, flushing, wanting to close my eyes entirely, but I'm too scared I'll fall if I do.

In my head, I see you — I see us — the way we were last night. I see your fiery eyes staring into mine. I feel

41

your one hand holding my wrists together over my head and against the mattress. I remember how my hands tightened and released in your grip.

"Not one word. Not one sound," you told me. "We don't want to wake anyone, do we?"

I shook my head. Your sister and her husband were asleep in their bedroom upstairs. You and I were supposed to be asleep on the futon in the family room. Instead, we were getting a little carried away. I knew you — knew us — and hoped your sister's bedroom door was closed.

You let go of my wrists and slid off the futon, standing up and motioning for me to follow. I sat up, but hesitated. Your face was in shadow, so I couldn't quite see your features, but I know you raised your eyebrows.

"Stand up." Your voice was quiet, but insistent. Commanding. I got off the futon and onto my feet.

"There," you said, pointing to a lit area of the bare wooden floor, a place where moonlight pouring through the window had drawn a parallelogram. You wanted me to stand there, so that is where I would stand. Walking the three feet from the futon, I felt clumsy and slow, like I was walking in sand.

"Take off the shirt."

I was wearing an oversized t-shirt, panties, and socks. I pulled the t-shirt off over my head and let it drop to the floor. I knew the room was chilly and that I should be cold, but I wasn't. I felt feverish. I always did.

I stood, facing you, unsure where to put my hands, where to look. You took my shoulders and moved me left, forward, right. You turned me away from the door to the hall and the stairs. And then you pulled my panties down over my hips. They fell to my feet. I didn't step out of them because you didn't tell me to step out of them. You didn't tell me to move, so I didn't. I stood there. Naked, except for socks. Waiting.

"Now, bend over."

"Should I hand them down or toss them to you?"

I've managed to dislodge an apple from the tree. I always forget how to pick apples at first, but then it comes back to me. Roll the apple up and twist until the stem pops loose. I have to think that, for me to know this, I must have been better about heights when I was younger. My parents must have sent me up apple trees just like these. Or maybe it was preschool and those shorter trees.

"Just drop them to me."

I don't want to go any farther up the ladder. I don't even want to lean too far away from the ladder, so there aren't many apples I can reach from here. You know that I'm scared of heights. But it's not all about the apples, is it? I find another apple within reach and twist it free.

"Catch!"

I drop an apple. You catch it with your other hand and drop it into the bag at your feet.

You run your hand up the back of my right calf, past the back of my knee, up beneath my skirt and along the backs of my thighs. You feel my legs shake, tiring from standing on the ladder in these shoes, tired of standing at all after last night.

We were interrupted. I was standing there in your sister's living room where you placed me, naked, bent over and gripping my ankles. I was exposed, my ass and pussy pointed toward the door. I swore to you I didn't need a gag, that I wouldn't make a noise. And I didn't make a noise at first. Not when you smacked me with the hairbrush the first time on my round bottom. Not the second time on the other cheek. Not until you hit me near where my ass meets my leg did I have to fight back a cry.

"Be quiet or I won't fuck you," you hissed. "You do want me to fuck you, don't you?"

"Yes."

And I did. It was clear I knew that before you slipped your hand between my legs and felt how I was dripping. Your cock slid easily into me. I could feel the heat of my reddening ass against your legs as you pushed in, pulled out. You grabbed my waist and pushed in again hard. And then… I yelped. I cried out as if we were at home, loud and unashamed, forgetting where we were.

"Are you two OK down there? Did you trip on something? Do you need me to find you a nightlight?"

"No, Sis. We're fine," you yelled, pulling out and motioning me back to the futon. We finished each other by hand, but… I knew you wouldn't forget it and that you would blame me for what happened. You would use it as an excuse — something that you could punish me for. So, basically, an excuse for fun.

I look down and see that you have both hands on my legs now. I'm not worried. I'm leaning forward on the ladder to push it against the tree, so it isn't going anywhere. But, with both hands on me, you don't have even one available when you hear me yell…

"Catch!"

I drop an apple before you're ready. The apple hits you square on the head. You back away from the ladder and look up at me, wondering if I did that on purpose. Maybe I did.

"Get down here."

"But we don't have a full bag yet."

"I said get down from the ladder. Now."

I don't give you an argument the second time. You've put on your Dom voice. I get down from the ladder.

"First you didn't listen to me last night. And now you hit me with an apple. I think we need to seriously continue last night's spanking. What do think?"

"Last night wasn't…" I stop.

"Lean against the ladder. Then pull your skirt up and your panties down. I'm going to find a nice switch…"

My face flushes and my stomach flutters. I look down at my feet, embarrassed by the knowledge that, not only am I about to do what you say, but that I desperately want to. I turn to face the ladder and place my hands on either side of the uprights. I hear your footsteps crackling in the fallen leaves. I look over my shoulder at you. The last of the light is silhouetting you so that you're as dark and long-shadowed as the trees in the orchard. Watching you, I think you could have forgotten me. As soon as the thought is formed, your head turns and catches me looking at you.

"I didn't tell you to watch me. I told you to pull up your skirt and bare your ass. Do that. Now."

My hands are clumsy and slow, but I do what I'm told. I pull my skirt up and tuck the back into the waistband. Then I pull my panties down over my ass. My legs are apart, so the panties don't fall. They stay there, suspended between my goosebumps and my knees.

"Bend over more."

I hear you coming up behind me. Your feet stop behind mine. You wrap your fingers in my hair and pull my head up and around so that I can see you.

45

"Lower."

You let go of my hair. I bend until my hands are braced on the second-lowest rung of the ladder. My ass is completely exposed and pushed high up into the air.

"Good girl," you say, rubbing my ass with the palm of your hand. Your hand feels warm and soft.

My breath comes fast and ragged. I am panting and trying to steel myself. But there's no way to prepare for the stinging blow when it comes — or the next or the ones that follow. There is the whistle in the air and then the quick hot sting of the switch landing. I try to find a way to breathe, but can only gasp from the pain.

"No, no, no. Stop!" It hurts so much that the words are out of my mouth before I want them to form.

Again, you grab my hair and pull my head straight back. You look directly into my eyes. "You. Do. Not. Tell. Me. No." You drop the switch onto the ground and slap my face. "Do you understand me?" My eyes water and I nod my head.

I hear you sigh as you bend over to pick up the switch. You move your feet and I close my eyes, anticipating the whine of the switch in the air as you start again.

"Count this time and thank me for each one."

It's dusk and the sky is growing dark. Well, not everywhere. The sun is setting behind you, so there's a little light by which to aim the switch as it falls on my ass again. I try to imagine what my flesh looks like from where you stand. In this light, my white skin must be bluish except where it has already been struck. There the streaks would be a peculiar purple. The streaks cross the bruises from last night's spanking in a criss-cross pattern. A bruise hedgehog. You swing the switch. Ow!

"One. Thank you."

My voice is cracking. Again, you swing the switch, aiming for an area you haven't touched yet. Ow! Fuck.

"Two. Thank you."

I feel your frustration. We're getting nowhere here or at least nowhere near where you want to be. This time, I'm guessing you'll aim for where the streaks are the darkest. You want the switch to hit me where I'm already hurt. You want this next one to be painful, so you'll swing the switch hard. I can picture it. I know it's coming. I breathe in and hold my breath, waiting for the switch to arc.

"Ahhh!"

The pain immediately causes my hand to come off the ladder and reach back to cover my ass with an outward facing palm. My hand rubs my ass with the knuckles.

"Put your hand back on the ladder, Nicole. Now. Unless you want me to hit that, too." You swish the stick through the air near my side. I flinch, but slowly I put my hand back up onto the ladder. You rearrange my skirt so that my ass is totally uncovered again.

"I think you forgot to thank me for that last one," you say, as you gently run your fingers over my warm and tingly skin. The stripes are raised slightly. That last one may have actually broken the skin. "I think we need to start over."

"No!" My head whips around, but my hands don't come off the ladder. "I mean..."

Slowly, you step to my side. You bend down and take an apple from the bag. Again, you grab me by the hair and pull my head back so that you're looking at me. My eyes are full of tears. I want this over now. I need you to fuck me more than I need any more of this scene.

"Since you can't seem to manage saying what I ask you to say, I don't want to hear you say anything. Open

47

your mouth." I open my mouth a little. "More!" you say, pulling my hair hard. I cry out, opening my mouth wide enough for me to jam the apple between my teeth.

"There. That should do it. Does the little piggie have anything more to say?"

I shake my head, trying hard to catch my breath through my nose. I'm shivering. My legs are wobbling. I think I've almost had enough games.

"Good. Let go of the ladder and turn around."

I'm dizzy and my nose is running. Slowly, I turn toward you. My skirt falls, covering my ass again. I can taste the apple juice in my mouth, mixing with my saliva. Another minute and I'll be drooling. I hate drooling. The last time we tried a ring gag, I swore I'd never do it again. Until we did it again.

"Are you going to be good?"

I nod. You reach your hand up in front of my face. I open my mouth and let you take out the apple. I don't close my mouth completely. I'm panting — a rapid, soft, staccato chant. It's hard to describe the headspace I'm in. The pain. The submission. Those things swirl around me. And when they fade or when I find a moment of clarity to see through their fog, I realize how terribly embarrassed I am — but at the same time how happy I am — at how wet I've gotten. You have taken me so far so quickly. I've let you. And I can't help but close my eyes, swallow, and think about how desperately I want your cock inside me.

You point to the ground in front of you. I step towards you and kneel in the dirt amongst the rotten apples, looking up into your dark eyes. My hands are shaking, clumsy as I unsnap your pants and unzip the fly. You are so hard already, straining against the striped fabric of your boxers. I hear your breath quicken.

"Take it out and suck it."

I lick my dry lips and open my mouth wide to take all of you in. I feel my knees buckle a little as I draw my mouth tight around the length of you, then pull back slowly, licking soft and strong and slow all the way to the tip. Your hands are in my hair and you pull my mouth onto you again and again. You are so very hard now, and I can taste how close your orgasm must be.

"Enough." You pull your cock out of my mouth.

Before I can think to feel denied, you take my hands and pull me to my feet. I sway as you pull me towards a large wooden barrel that you see standing at the end of a tree row. You turn me to face the barrel. The barrel is turned over with the flat bottom facing up. Its wood is smooth and so is the raised rim formed by the side staves. You place your right hand on my shoulder and I respond to only the slightest hint of pressure. I bend over the barrel, resting my elbows on the flat wood and clutching the far rim with my hands. I can hear you breathing hard, but my head is down and my hair hides my face.

Slowly, you start to pull my skirt up again. Inch by inch, you pull it higher, letting me feel it crawl up the side of my legs, my thighs, closer and closer to my ass (which shifts from side to side in anticipation). You spread my feet apart a bit more. I'm still wearing my heels, now somewhat muddy.

Another inch and then another. Soon the cloth of my skirt rides up over the naked roundness of my ass. My panties? We may never find those again in this light. The old man will get a laugh out of them when he finds them tomorrow or the next day.

Even in the bluish twilight, I can see the stripes on my skin edging around the sides of my hips. I can't see their color, but I can feel the warm, raised flesh as you run your fingers and palms over the surface.

You gather the skirt cloth together and tuck it between my belly and the side of the barrel. My bare ass edges back to meet your palms. My head bows more, close to resting on the barrel between my hands. My fingers are gripping the wood tighter as one of your hands slips between my legs and your fingers slip into my too-honest wetness. I moan and shift my weight. My heels rise up off the backs of my shoes.

This part isn't a game. It isn't top or bottom. You're offering something for me to take before you take what I have to offer. Right now, you are offering me a way to scratch the itch, to put out the fire and light another. So, you don't move the hand between my legs. You don't move the fingers slipped so slickly into my folds. You leave them firm and steady, letting me rub myself against them. And I do, not waiting for anything more by way of invitation. I take. I grind on your hand, pushing you between my lips. I take, hitting my clit with your fingertips and soaking your hand.

I move faster, starting to cum, crying out into the dark hollow between my forearms, my chest, and the wood of the barrel. Then I remember that I don't have to be quiet out here and I tip my head back. Let the owl hear me. Owl, mice, leering old man. I don't care who hears me. My thighs quake as my abdomen spasms. The sounds I make aren't words.

That's when I hear you unbuckle your belt with your other hand. Your pants and boxers fall to your ankles. Gripping my shoulder with your other hand, you withdraw the hand between my legs and replace it with an eager, throbbing cock. My pussy is still fluttering, still contracting, when you slip inside me. I grip your cock and make some reference to popular deity as you start to move within me.

I look over my shoulder, though there's no way I can see more than a hint of you, thrusting behind me. What I can see, what I notice when I turn my head, is how the shadow of us fucking reaches across the road and into the trees. The sun is so low on the horizon now that our shadow stretches on and on, tens of yards. Our shadow legs are like bars in the dirt. Your shadow shape moves against my shape and the barrel's shape on the trunks of the Cortland trees. We're like shadow puppets and this shadow play won't end until we're both standing here, spent and dripping cum.

"I don't know about you," you say, smiling as we walk back to our car. "But I'm absolutely starving." I immediately think of a warm fireplace, waiters bringing wine and food, and perhaps chairs with seats made of cool, smooth leather for my sensitive posterior.

I reach into the half-filled bag and pull out an apple. I make a show of polishing it on my blouse before putting it up to your mouth. You smile. And then you open your mouth, bite into the apple, and I let it go.

"There you go, my sweet piggie," I say, patting your cheek. "Something to tide you over."

Colorforms

"Pose for me."

I said it on a whim. Part of what appealed to me in the instant was the light in the room. Sunlight was spilling in through the windows. It wasn't the soft, pink light we normally have at sunrise or the golden light of sunset. It was the harsh, mid-morning light of summer, the light that promises — OK, threatens — that by afternoon the temperatures in the apartment will be soaring and you won't want to be touched by the sun — or anyone or anything else — at all.

But somehow, the light that morning wasn't harsh at all. Once it was through the window, the light's mood was changed by whatever it struck, covered, bounced off. On the wooden floor, it became calm and earthen. On the off-white walls, it looked like a warm, flannel blanket. It played with the primary colors of the glass knickknacks on the shelves. And when the light touched your skin? Well, that was the other thing that appealed to me.

Just out of the shower, you were standing there in the sunlight, drying your auburn hair with a turquoise towel. A dozen drops of water you had missed sparkled and shined like jewels on your shoulders and back. Your skin glowed like backlit alabaster. And when you bent over to let your hair hang down so that you could wrap the towel around it, the sun reflecting off the wooden floor shined through that gap where your legs meet your torso — and the hair there looked fiery red.

"What did you say?" you said, straightening up and adjusting the towel.

"I said 'Pose for me.' I want to draw you."

"I'd like to, but I just washed mah hair." You opened your eyes wide and batted your eyelashes.

I smiled. "You realize I'm probably the only person you know who's actually watched that movie. Have you seen it?"

"Absolutely. I binge-watched ten Bette Davis movies in ten nights between sophomore and junior years. I was partial to the early, blonde Bette."

"Pose for me."

"Right now?" you asked, smiling.

"Yes, right now. This light is great and you look sexy wonderful." Pause. "And besides, you're already naked. Points for that. "

"I am, aren't I?" You feigned looking at your belly and ass, smiling.

"Yes. So pose for me! Besides, you're always giving me shit for having all of my old art supplies around the apartment when I never use them anymore."

"You don't use them anymore. When was the last time you took an art class?" Innocent blinking.

"I know. Fine. So, pose for me and we can have our own art class today. That will justify my hoarding paper and charcoal for the next couple of years." I smiled. "Great plan or what?"

"OK, OK. Not sure what's in it for me..."

"Immortality."

You laugh. "Where do you want me, Matisse?"

You pulled the towel off your hair and threw it toward the bathroom where it landed with a muted, damp thump. You stood with one leg slightly bent and all your weight on the other, fluffing up your hair so that it would dry more quickly.

I watched your breasts move bounce, jiggle, sway. I thought, "I don't usually know models' breasts as well as I know these breasts." I wasn't sure whether, in terms of the drawing, that was a good thing or bad. Would I draw a breast differently if I knew its heft or its internal texture? You cleared your throat, dislodging me from my breast reverie. I looked up and found you looking at me, eyebrows raised, head tilted to the side.

"Right. Where should you be?" I looked around. "I like this natural light from the window for you, so you should be somewhere over here." I pointed over toward where our bikes were propped along the long wall in the living room. "If you're there, then I can sit over here where there's light from the kitchen. And..." I looked around again. "Yeah, that'll work. You should just stand on the coffee table. We can move the bikes and then move the coffee table to where the bikes are."

"Got it," you said, starting to wheel a bike into the hallway. "You gather your art supplies and I'll move the bikes and table. Nude interior design. Fanny shui. It could be the next big thing." You were out of sight, but I heard you add, "The service. Not my fanny."

I found my drawing board with its pad of newsprint drawing paper propped up behind a chair in the bedroom. The loose sheets of pastel paper were harder to get at. I had taped them between two pieces of matte board and stuck them in the closet. Luckily, all of my other art supplies — my pencils, charcoal, pastels, blending stumps, erasers — were in a wooden tackle box on a shelf in the bedroom. I brought everything into the kitchen and pulled up a chair before arranging my materials so that they were within reach. You were pushing the coffee table away from the couch. Your hair was mostly dry by then, but your skin somehow still looked pink and fresh-scrubbed, recently toweled.

"I'm gonna put on some music." My laptop was on the dining table, between the kitchen area and what passed as our living room. I opened a radio app and let it create a quick, classical music station. No more than ten seconds of "Eine Kleine Nachtmusik" played before you stopped what you were doing and shot me a look.

"Really? Is that what they play in figure drawing classes?" At college, you had satisfied your Arts concentration with a class called "Women, The Vulva, and the Secret History of Western Art," so it wasn't as if you had ever needed to set foot in an actual studio. You could, however, spot a symbolic vagina from 100 paces.

"No," I answered. "Those classes are usually silent except for the sounds of people drawing and shifting on their stools. And maybe the sound of the art teacher berating me for drawing what I saw instead of painting what I felt." Obviously, I wasn't a big fan of college art teachers.

You smiled. "Please change the music. I get that you don't want me dancing. And we both know we can't have a conversation without me moving my hands. So find some music that will keep us awake and focused. Not Mozart or Chopin."

"Sure. I'll try for something more contemporary." I searched for Bix Beiderbecke, hit the Play button, and the tinny, lo-tech sounds of 1920s jazz filled the room. You scrunched your face at me. "Hey, I said 'more contemporary.' At least this is *slightly* less than 100 years old."

I sat down in the hardback kitchen chair, opened my box of art supplies, and took out a gray envelope filled with different types of charcoal. I took out a long, slender piece of twig charcoal and tucked it into a crease of my boxers. It would do. I could always get out other charcoal or conte crayons or maybe pastels later, if things went well and we didn't lose interest.

The drawing board was still on the floor, leaning against the kitchen table. I picked it up, rested the bottom edge on my lap, and held the top steady with my left hand as I turned the pad to a blank sheet of newsprint. I looked around the board from the right side to see if you were ready.

The coffee table was about a foot and a half off the ground, but was made of good, solid oak with thick, even legs that I knew wouldn't wobble. So, although you stepped up onto the table tentatively, you soon felt comfortable to move around.

"What would you like me to do?" you asked, first waving at me, then making jazz hands. "How about this?" you asked, holding your breasts up and out with your hands like a pose from a 1950s girlie magazine. The pouting lips were thankfully three degrees short of a duckface.

"Um, no," I said. "I don't think so. I think your boobs should chill and be themselves. For now, we're just going to do some quick poses. I'll tell you when to change. Just vary which way you're facing, how your torso turns... Right? Twist. Bend. I won't have you hold any pose too long, so you can do fun, weird things as long as you don't fall over and need stitches."

We started with quick poses of three minutes each, timed with the small sand timer I took from your Boggle set. The idea of gesture drawing is to capture the basic form of the model's pose and to convey the mood, action, and distribution of weight in a simple set of quickly-drawn lines. Gesture drawings can be done with poses as short as 10 or 15 seconds. But switching poses that quickly takes a model with more experience and I wasn't interested in that kind of exercise. A few three minute poses would get us both warmed up to what we were doing.

At first, you stood straight and still, a three-quarters pose that put your right breast and your face in partial profile. I picked up the twig charcoal from my lap and began to draw. In just three minutes, all I would have time for would be to draw lines for your head, your hair, the curve of your back on one side, your stomach on the other. This was a pose about twisting and that's what my lines showed.

There was no more sand in the timer. "Time's up! Change poses."

In the next pose, you stood sideways and bent down as if to touch your toes. Your hair, still damp, hung down and brushed the tabletop. I sketched slowly at first, but then faster and with more confidence. The charcoal in my hand moved faster over the newsprint, drawing lines as before, but this time scrubbing in gray shapes to suggest the mass of your shoulders, the draping of your hair.

Again, the timer ran out. "New pose!"

Next you lunged forward with your right leg, as if you were fencing. I picked up a larger stick of charcoal so that I could use broad strokes of black to capture the essence of the lines I saw in your body. No matter how angular your pose, I saw everything as a series of arcs and curves, similarities of form and scale, the curve under your chin something like the curve under your breasts, the forearm like your upper thigh.

Several other poses followed in quick succession. In one, you turned away from me and leaned against the wall so that I could draw you from behind. In another, you stretched toward the ceiling with both hands and I watched as your underboobs disappeared. Each time the pose changed, I would flip my drawing pad to a clean sheet of paper, turn over the sand timer, and begin again. There's that arc again. There's your center of gravity.

I called for the next pose. I looked away from you long enough to reset the timer. When I looked back at you, I saw that you were crouched down as if you were a catcher in a baseball game. Your bent legs were spread wide apart and you rested your arms on your knees. You were on your toes, so that there was a quiver as you fought to hold still.

I quickly started drawing, seeing the lines, drawing the lines, trying to express the tension and the balance. In this pose, I could see your labia peeking out from your pubic hair as if sticking out a tongue. But this was the wrong scale to draw that. I made two quick slashes with the charcoal and moved on to your calves.

Something about you was different. I could tell you were staring at me, studying me. "Hey, Mr. Rembrandt!" you said. You teetered slightly, but held the pose.

"Just another minute. Time's almost up." I kept drawing. If I didn't get to your feet on the table, what would support all of these lines in space?

"I was just thinking," you started, still squatting in place on the table. "Aside from the fact that I'm naked and flashing you my bits before I've even had breakfast,

I'm working pretty hard here. It seems to me that the least you could do is get a boner!"

I laughed. You didn't know what I was or wasn't drawing. But you could see where I was and wasn't looking. So, if I was looking at your pussy and not getting excited, that was bad. If I wasn't looking at your pussy, that was bad, too. The thing was, I had an explanation, but there wasn't much of a chance you would buy it.

"Sweetie, it's not you. I don't think I've done that since the first time I saw a nude model in freshman year. And I've had a lot of figure drawing classes since then."

"Why not? Here's a real naked woman, only a few feet away. Tits! Ass! Vag!"

The sand timer ran out. "Time's up. You can stand up." Instead, you shifted to get one foot out from under you and then the other. You sat on the edge of the table, facing me.

You still had your legs spread apart, flashing me, and I admit my eyes wandered there as I spoke. "OK, here's the thing. Art instructors go out of their way to teach art students to draw what they see, not what they think they see. You learn to boil the object down to simple shapes. After a while, all you see are the lines, not the actual thing. It's not a table; it's a set of straight lines and planes. It's not a naked woman; it's cylinders and spheres and arcs."

"Well, that's stupid." You have an endearing way of calling things the way you see them.

I smiled. "Yeah, I know. Seems like a waste of a perfectly good naked woman." Out of habit, I started to wipe the charcoal from my hands onto my pants, but I wasn't wearing any pants. I had been drinking coffee and reading when you came out of the shower, so I was just wearing a t-shirt and my boxers. I put down the charcoal and the drawing board, got up from the chair, and walked into the kitchen to grab a dishtowel. It was almost laundry day and we had another, so I used the dishtowel to wipe the charcoal from my hands.

"Can we do a longer pose?" I asked you. The light was still good and you didn't look tired so much as... challenged.

"Sure. But you're taking me for pancakes after."

"Of course." You wanted to go to Dinerella. You always have the chocolate-chip pancakes. I often have the stuffed French toast. "That's really helping my concentration, by the way."

"Really? The thought of brunch food that's not presently here is more distracting to you than boobs that are here? That's it. We need counseling." You laughed. I knew you meant that, except for the counseling part.

I took a piece of the pastel paper from the kitchen table and attached it to my drawing board, rough side up. I had chosen a dark brown piece of charcoal paper to work with. It would be good because of the light. Using light pastels on a dark paper would let me show how the light streamed across the floor and slashed across the wall behind you. It would help me show the way your body was glowing.

I sat back down and bent over to dig through the box of art supplies at my feet. I threw the pieces of charcoal back inside and dug for the box of pastels. "When was the last time I used these?" I thought to myself. College? Maybe that time Laura hired a model and had friends over to her apartment to drink wine and draw?

I picked up the drawing board and a couple of pastels. "OK, I'm about ready. Do you have a pose you can hold for... oh, maybe 20 minutes?"

"I think I'm good where I am," you replied.

I looked around the drawing board so that I could see you again. You were still sitting on the edge of the table, facing me, the way you were before. But your left arm had moved off to your side and back. That hand was flat on the tabletop and that arm supported you as you leaned back slightly. Your right hand rested on the upper part of your right thigh. Your shoulders were squared, your back straight, and your chest out. A band of sunlight lit one breast, but missed the other entirely.

Your legs were spread apart at the knees but came back together again where the soles of your feet faced and almost touched each other on the sunlit floor. And when you knew I was looking, you spread your legs apart wider still. It was as much a display or a show as it was a pose. I could see everything. And the way you were staring at me, I knew that was clearly your intention. "OK," I thought. "So this might not be a drawing we put on the refrigerator for friends to see."

I started to draw. I made a broad sweep with the side of a pale yellow pastel and slashed in the sun that I could see on the floor. Next, I drew in the basic presence of the table using brown pastel, lighter than the brown of the paper. There — something to support you.

Then I started to draw you. I decided to go with a middle tone first, so I grabbed a peach pastel and roughed in your basic shape, filling it in to make a solid mass. I used the side of my thumb to smear and blend the pastel until it was smooth. Then I went back with a salmon pastel and added darker color. Volume started to emerge — the shading from the second color suggesting the roundness and weight of your breasts, the hollows at the base of your neck, the splaying outward of your legs.

I quickly roughed in the shape of your hair with a dark brown pastel, knowing that I would want to go back later and add more colors. I added a few quick touches with the brown pastel to the edges of your body and blended them in to form the darkest shadows. The dish towel was a mess now, as I kept using my thumb to blend the pastels and then the towel to clean off my thumb.

Next, I worked back the other way: light to lighter. I found a pastel called "bisque" that was lighter than the peach. I used bisque to suggest the places where the sunlight was playing across your body. I drew in the shapes. I was interested in how the sunlight came in through the window in straight lines and then was translated to curves as it fell across your breasts, your belly, your upper legs.

Then came white. I took a white pastel and started to put in the highlights. I smiled. I was happy with how the drawing was turning out. Each new tone I added got me closer to recreating the volume of you, the space you filled, and how lovely you looked, glowing in the sun.

What next? I looked at you, this time with my eyes set to look at smaller features instead of the big shapes and forms. Then I looked back at my drawing. I needed to shade in your right hand, give you nipples, pubic hair… eventually make my way back to your head and your face. It was time to start working on details.

But when I looked up at you again, a detail had changed. Your hand had moved. It was only a few inches… not so much as to move your whole body or even the upper part of your arm. But your right hand had moved from the top of your leg… to between your legs.

Your palm rested on the lower part of your belly, covering much of your patch of hair. The thumb pointed out and toward your left side. The index finger lazily rested on the inside of your left upper thigh. The other three fingers were there between your legs, hovering, waiting as if part of the pose.

I grabbed several pastel colors from the box and tried to sketch in the details of what I saw. You couldn't see my erection growing behind the drawing board.

You had been waiting to catch me looking. You began to slowly move your middle and ring fingers down and back along your vulva. It was almost imperceptible at first. The fingers moved in and back out with little more than a slight bending of the knuckles. Your hand didn't move at all. Just the fingers. Bending, dipping.

I quickly tried to finish the drawing. I found a dark rose pastel for your nipples which were hardening noticeably as I drew them. Pubic hair that I could see, those fingers again… quickly now, trying to get some details down on paper. But when I went to start on your face, I looked up to find your eyes looking straight into my eyes. I could see you breathing. I drew your mouth, open slightly.

Your fingers started to move faster and with more freedom. You spread your legs a little more and I could see your fingers sliding along your labia. "What color are those?" I thought. Fuck.

I unclipped the drawing from the drawing board and dropped the paper on the floor as I got up and moved to the kitchen table to grab another piece of pastel paper. I quickly clipped the fresh paper to the board. I looked back at you, still sitting in your pose on the table. Your whole hand was moving now, but still not your arm, not your body.

Carrying the drawing board, I dragged my chair to the middle of the room, halving the distance between us. I kicked the box of supplies over to the chair and sat down.

I was only about six feet away from you now. Your eyes were slightly closed, but still looking at me. I could see your pink tongue licking the corner of your mouth. I picked up a pastel and started drawing again.

At first, I tried to draw everything from your breasts to your knees, but my eyes kept coming back to your pussy. I saw your fingers spreading your labia apart, exposing folds and wet-slick colors. So I quickly grabbed the whole box of pastels and tried to get down on paper all the colors I was seeing. Salmon, coral, light pink, light violet red. The middle of the paper was covered with multiple images of your vulva: the roundness of the outside, the petal-like inside surfaces that your fingers were exposing. Not one drawing was the same as the one next to it. You were changing that rapidly.

I edged my chair even closer to you. I was now maybe three feet away. Although I was still drawing, now you could see my cock, which had found its way outside of my boxers and was bobbing in midair.

You slipped two fingers into your pussy. When you drew them back out, they were shiny and wet. And then you pushed them back inside, deeper.

Soon you were alternating. First, you circled your fingers on your clit. Then you plunged two fingers into your pussy while shaking your hand back and forth. Circle, circle, circle ... shake shake shake shake. Circle, circle, circle ... shake shake shake. Inside, outside, back inside, fucking yourself with those two fingers, moving them in and out of you the way I wanted to. But I was still trying my best to draw what I was seeing.

And the colors! The colors were changing in real time. Your labia had grown thicker from the blood — all darker and deeper in color. Now the colors were pale violet red, orchid, magenta, maroon. And when your fingers spread your lips apart again, I saw deep pink— not the garish pink of rhododendrons, but more like the color of pink tulips. I had the box of pastels in my lap, but couldn't keep up with finding the pastels as I needed them. So many colors!

I found that the faster you went, the more slowly I could draw. I was barely able to take my eyes off the colors, your fingers flying sliding probing shaking circling flicking thrusting...

And then you came.

Your upper body lurched forward as your stomach muscles tensed. You pulled your legs together around your hand, which was still moving on your clit, your fingers still sliding in and out. You gasped for air and rocked a little from side to side. "Unnhhhhhhh..." Your head hung forward and your breathing was fast and shallow, then eventually slow, long, and deep. A red flush spread over your chest like spilled ink as the waves passed over you and withdrew.

I got up from my chair, put down the drawing board and the pastels, and took the two short steps to where you were sitting on the table, holding your knees to your chest and rocking back and forth. I reached out to touch your hair. Your hand, still wet, reached up to touch my hand. And when you looked up at me, we were both smiling.

You were aware of my cock before you actually looked at it. But there it was, right in front of your face: hard and purple, so full of blood that it stuck straight out through the opening in my boxers and bobbed up and down with the beat of my pulse.

The thing was, my balls ached with having watched you. So it wasn't any surprise that I came soon after you pulled my boxers down, grabbed my ass with both hands to pull me to you, and wrapped your warm mouth around the head of my cock. A few bobs, a few circles with your tongue, and my knees buckled.

What was surprising was that, no sooner had I come and you had sucked me dry, you pointed me to the patch of floor still in the sun and climbed on top of me as soon as my ass hit the floor. The surprise was that I was inside you before there was even a chance for my erection to go away. Maybe it wouldn't have. Maybe I was too excited to just let it go at that.

But there I was, inside you, feeling and watching you move above me. I reached up to hold your breasts, circling the hard nipples with my thumbs, suspending the weight of your breasts with my hands as you moved your body up and down. My pastel-covered thumbs left deep pink smudges wherever I touched.

You squatted, straddling me, up on your toes. And with each downward bounce that you made, the force drove me deep inside you. You moved faster and faster, sometimes pushing off of my chest, sometimes pushing off of your own knees with your hands. Faster and harder.

"Yeah! Oh, yeah! That's so good!" You took one hand off my chest and brushed the hair back from your face. Your cheeks were pink, the same way they get when you've been out for a run.

There was no doubt that I wanted to be there with you on that floor, fucking between art and brunch. But there was still a small part of me — artist or voyeur, I can't say which — that wanted to also be sitting across the room, watching us fucking and drawing us fucking, trying without regret or success to find the right shapes and the right colors.

I looked down along my chest, past my belly, and I could see your pussy swallowing my cock, coming down on it like a falling elevator, then pulling back up with your lips pulling out around it. We were fucking in one of the polygons of sunlight on the floor. My backlit cock had edges shiny like glass. Your hair and my hair? The hair around our lips and our cock, the hair that merged and parted, again and again? The drops and strings of liquid on our hair sparkled in the light that found its way between us.

You pounded at me, riding me into the wooden floorboards. I tried to push up with my legs, tried to arch my back and raise myself off the floor, but again and again you drove me back down. Your pussy contracted around me on the upstroke, let go on the down stroke, pulling up, dropping down. Each time the head of my cock hit your cervix, my hip bones dug into my ass from the inside out. It wasn't painful. But it felt as if, with every impact, shock waves radiated from my hip bones, went through me, then joined together on the other side — amplified — and moved through my cock and into you.

I could feel myself starting to come again. It was there, just beyond the horizon and approaching like a maglev bullet train. I looked into your eyes and saw that you already knew. I slid my right hand between us and placed my thumb at the base of my cock where your clit would hit the knuckle. I knew that would be enough.

You came before I did, pausing on the down stroke, dropping from your toes to your knees, your legs shuddering on either side of my hips. I kept pumping into you. You collapsed forward and your breasts grazed my chest. And then you started moving on me again. Your face was just above mine and we locked eyes as I grabbed your hips and pulled you down, thrusting deep inside you as the spasms rolled through me.

I hugged you to my chest and we rocked from side to side, me still inside you, you still contracting involuntarily around me as your climax tapered off. We kissed, our tongues slipping around each other. You bit my lower lip so hard that I thought you surely must have drawn blood. I wanted to smack your ass in retaliation, but thought better of it. I wanted you there on top of me. That's all I wanted. That's all I've ever wanted.

It was about that time that one of my drawings caught your eye. It was lying on the floor about a foot from our heads. You rolled off to my side and got up on one elbow. You scooted the drawing closer with the other hand and looked at it thoughtfully.

"This is pretty. Did my pussy really look like this?"

"This time. Other times, it looks ... more relaxed."

"Which do you prefer?"

"I think we should discuss that after pancakes." I got to my feet and pulled on my boxers before helping you stand. "I have some ideas for a different pose."

The Distance Dance

Wednesday, July 6, 1983

Dear Nell,

Hello, old salt. I was walking down Route 4 yesterday, down near the bridge over West Hickman Creek, and I noticed that the crepe myrtle is in bloom. The air was thick with it, Nell — rich, bitter, red-berry ripe. Maybe that's why I thought of you and that time we both went walking down by Mad Dog Denkman's farm.

The road wasn't paved then and the bridge was only wide enough for one car. Mad Dog was building a house of cedar wood and we wanted to see it first-hand. So, we packed some seedless grapes in a knapsack and set out on foot. The house was an hour's walk down an old, dry creek bed and up the hill a ways. We finished the grapes long before we got to the house, breathless, our clothes soaked through with sweat.

That afternoon, while the grasshoppers in the field made a noise like a Weedeater, we made love in front of Mad Dog's unlit hearth. Nothing stopped. No one noticed. The grasshoppers went on with their sawing. The red berries continued ripening and the gnats dashed around our heads like thin, grey halos.

There was sawdust in your hair and sawdust pressed into my elbows, my knees. We came at the same time, and it made us laugh. "Just like in the books, huh?" We rubbed the puddle into the wood, but it didn't stain. We agreed sex should always be that way — with nature all around: in our noses, our ears, painfully pressed into our elbows… Crepe myrtle.

Maybe that's also why I dreamed about you last night. In my dream, we were standing on a natural rock bridge, our feet resting on sandstone carved by hundreds of thousands of years of wind. I smiled to think that the initials of lovers, carved there since the invention of pocketknives and inconsideration, would be gone in the blink of a geologic timescale eye. Beneath the bridge? A void. To the left and right, there stretched a valley filled with green pines and autumn-colored maples. Somewhere down there was a river. Our bare toes played on a frozen beach.

You stood there with me, your hair blowing south as you smiled east. On your left arm, perched a raven. On your right arm, a dove. Without sound, they flew off, circling below us, flying beneath the bridge and into the valley. We were naked in my dream, and the wind on the bridge made the hair on our forearms stand on end. Your nipples stood out so much that I wanted to place a Life Saver on each one, flesh filling hole.

I stretched out on the rock. Placed just so, we could have used the shadow of my erection in the sun to tell time. You sat on my stomach. I could feel the coolness of your ass on my thighs. A certain hardness tapped in the crease with each pulsing heartbeat. Time was stretching, too; even the wind in the trees had lost all noise.

For a time, I helped your breasts beat gravity, holding them aloft with my hands: supporting, cupping, rubbing

70

circles with my thumbs. When my hands wandered down, you smiled and leaned your head back, face up to the sky. I curled your pubic hair about my fingers — tight pin curls, neatly arranged. I couldn't see anything but hair, not even with my chin pressed into my chest. But I felt pink with my thumb — wet pink, warm pink. I thought I could hear the river.

It was nighttime when you moved back and took me inside you. The moon had risen, and it seemed to rest on your left shoulder like the head of a baby. I felt tides rippling, washing over me, gripping me and letting me go. Muscles you didn't even know you had pulled me inside; desires I didn't know I had spread out and latched on. Leaning forward, your hair fell around me like a veil. Slowly, we moved. Slowly, I felt each grain of sand pluck itself free of the rock bridge and fly off into the black. Soon we would be floating in space.

It was dawn when I felt the coming rush. I said, "Nell, stop moving. Stop the world. Stop the continental plates, the traffic, the noise. Stop everything! It can be so wonderful if you'll just stop! Nell, if you'll just stop for a second, I can inhabit you and never come out."

But you replied, "I can't stop. Don't you stop. Keep moving. Deeper, if you can. Don't stop! If you just keep moving, I know we can vibrate into another plane!"

Between the moving and the stopping, between living and dying, we came. We came like earthquakes, shaking violently, then quivering with aftershocks. We came like lava waterfalls; we came like ice-water geysers and bursting dams. We came like the cry of eagles, like the pleased coo of a baby soiling his diaper. We came like a burst of cold air in a Louisiana swamp. We came like someone expecting a surprise.

We came, but we never arrived. You exploded into an ocean of lilacs; I melted into a stream of flowing stone. The flowers floated upon the liquid, suspended, pendulous, then dipping in with lips like seabirds, diving, fishing for other lips. From the petals, a hand emerged, then a face, then both breast and arm. Rock once became stone again and you placed the remaining flowers upon me, a wreath upon a maypole. And there you danced, a ring of light and water, until I awoke, hard as in my dreams.

Nell, you're a pebble in my shoe. If this letter finds you, then maybe so can I.

With ever-growing fondness,
Max

Thursday, July 28, 1983

Dear Nell,

OK, so now I can't take a shower anymore without laughing. I hope you're satisfied, you fiend. Just this morning, I got up and stumbled into the bathroom the way I always do — without glasses, absent-mindedly scratching my balls, stepping into the tub with my left foot first, pulling the curtain, turning on the water and bending over to test it with my fingers (having once again found my toes untrustworthy). My eyes were barely open, Nell, and yet I found myself laughing as soon as I heard the water come through the nozzle, felt it hit my head and drip down my stomach. I can't help it. Friday night was ridiculous.

It's these summers, isn't it? They keep driving us back to the water. Two years ago, it was the plunge pool beneath the abandoned falls at Jennings Branch. The water was clear and cold as snow, and minnows swam around your breasts like silver satellites. Beneath the water, the limestone ledge we sat on was covered with mossy green algae, so wet and slick that I began to think maybe you were lined with algae, all green inside instead of pink. I was sitting on algae; you were sitting on me, covering me with algae. I felt as if I were becoming part of the ledge. I thought, "This must be what it was like to make love in the Paleozoic."

And it's nice to know Non-Oxynol 9 also kills freshwater organisms. At least, that's what I imagine.

Again, back to water. Do you think the bathtub in my old apartment was wider than this one? Not that making love in that tub was without humor, as you no doubt remember. This was last summer. We had just gotten back from the softball game, sticky with sweat. A shower sounded wonderful. You were out of your t-shirt and bra before I even got to the bathroom, closing the door behind me, and turning out the light.

It was late afternoon and the sunlight coming in through the plastic window curtain over the tub made the room swim in a grassy green. I grabbed you by the waistband and, sitting down on the toilet, began to take off your shorts — brass button, zipper. Then I got distracted, feeling a need to run my green hands up your inner leg, letting two green fingers slip inside the green cloth of your shorts I rubbed you through your sweat-drenched panties and finally pulled the shorts down over green hips and dropped them to the floor. You held my head to your chest and I licked salt from beneath each breast.

As I undressed, you sat on the sink, legs apart, feet swinging, kicking the cabinet over and over, showing me some bit of color, an exclamation point in shades of magenta and rose. My erection nodded with my pulse — and it was green, too.

You were on your back, legs drawn up. I was on top of you, feet pushed up against the end of the tub, hands on the rim, my back an umbrella. Water from the shower dripped from my shoulders into your mouth. It ran down the crack in my ass and pooled between your legs.

All around us, the green seemed to get darker and deeper — the color of malachite. Our breathing began to sound like hard rain falling on green leaves. We wrapped ourselves together like vines.

I was so carried away by the time I came, I was nearly driving your head into the faucet with each thrust. "We'll have to switch ends next time," you said afterward.

That was then. Now, here it is, summer once again. And Friday night, we were so hot after our walk that we had taken to fanning each other with album covers. When you mentioned that we should take a shower, I was on my feet in seconds, leaving a trail of clothing from the living room to the bathroom.

When you came in, I already had the shower turned on, the water cooler than lukewarm. You turned out the light and stepped into the tub. The bathroom was almost completely dark. I followed your lead; I followed your scent. You told me to sit, so I sat in the tub, my back to the drain. The water from the shower was hitting me in the back of the head, rushing over my hair and running into my eyes and nose.

You sat, straddling me, and together we maneuvered until I was inside you. Your legs were pressed into my sides; my legs were pinned against the tub. When we started moving, it became obvious that the fit was too snug to be practical. We couldn't move. When we tried, the water pooled between our stomachs shot up between your breasts like a geyser, spraying both our chins. "And

74

they found them there, wedged into the tub, having died from starvation." We fell into laughter and each other's arms, my erection fading and withdrawing. Another time.

I've thought of that every time I've taken a shower this week. And that's why you're a fiend.

Of course, that wasn't the end. After we dried off and poured ourselves some lemonade, we began kissing, naked on the couch. The floor fan moved back and forth like a watchful dog. I took an ice cube from my glass and placed it against your bare skin. Starting at your chin and coming down your throat, the melting ice spilled drops of water down your stomach and sides. You shivered and took in such a sharp breath of air when I touched your nipples with the ice that I thought your back would break. When I put my tongue on one of them, the nipple was cool and hard as a pill.

You sipped at your lemonade. Taking ice into your mouth, you lowered your head to my lap and took me into your mouth. Hot and cold. I could feel your tongue reading unknown braille on the head of my cock.

We made love on the coffee table, resplendent with its fake wood Formica top. In the background, the floor fan droned on, all white noise and artificial breeze. The Mets were playing the Giants on television; but with the sound off and my glasses on the armchair, the game was just another square of dancing colors.

You know I like it that you've grown your hair long again. As I slipped into you and felt that familiar tug and grip, I saw your hair spilling over the end of the table like a dark waterfall. These old knees of mine wouldn't take kneeling on the table, so I straddled it, and moved up and down, rocking on my toes, in and out of your sunset, your question, your every answer.

Nell, it's true that I may crack a smile about us whenever I'm in the shower. But I'm going to try to keep a straight face about the coffee table. No matter what, entertaining in the living room will definitely never be the same. People will set their glasses of sweet tea where your head once was; I'll place trays of crackers and cheese where we drew a spider from our pond of sap.

My god, Nell, but you're everywhere these days.

Still in you,
Max

Monday, August 22, 1983

Dear Nell,

You forgot to take your diaphragm with you again. After you left this morning, I found it on the back of the toilet, still slightly soggy from washing. They really are the silliest looking things. Trampolines for mice. Hamster Frisbees. Are they all this bland beige color, or do some manufacturers have fun with them, making "party colors" the way they do with condoms? I wonder. Doctors have some say in these things, and we all know they haven't a funny bone in their bodies. Prescription for Nell: one mid-sized diaphragm, Passion Pink. I can't see it, either.

As usual, I let it air by the window — by the jar of dried flowers — for an hour or so. I never know how long it will be until you come to see me again, so every time I find myself dusting this thing with cornstarch before putting it into its blue case and putting it away. Someone told me that's what you do with diaphragms. I didn't just make this up, did I?

Taking care of it, I try to think that it's a part of you. On loan, some piece from inside you, something I've touched, something that sometimes has nerve endings and quivers when touched. I have felt it in place. With my fingers, I've felt it, warm and slippery inside you. And sometimes, when you're on top of me, I can feel the head of my cock hitting a wall that gives. It's a terribly male thing to say, Nell, but when that happens, I feel adequate in a strictly… equipment sort of way.

So, it's in the medicine chest now, next to the soap we stole from the Howard Johnson's in Gatlinburg last November and that piss-poor salve for poison ivy. It'll be there when you return. I only wonder why it is the tube of spermicide never stays behind, too. I think I approve of the mixed message.

Not that you care, but my sheets may never be the same. I tried scrubbing them this afternoon, but I don't think the chocolate sauce is going to come out. Granted, I can't think of a nobler sacrifice for a piece of cloth to make. And it was fun, wasn't it?

Nell, there was a time when I was seeing all of that in slow motion — the dark, sweet sauce running down the curves of your breasts, down the slope of your rib cage… and when you breathed out, overtaking your stomach and pooling in your navel. And when I started a second flood at your navel, pouring sauce down from there and over your belly, there were rippling crescendos of chocolate. They hit your bush, backed up, then eased through. I wish you could have seen it (maybe this is a good reason for a convenient hand mirror?), but the vividness of color — the pink of your labia contrasted against the near-black of the chocolate — made me want to freeze the moment on canvas or film. Instead, I accepted it as free dessert.

You'll always taste of chocolate to me now. It took so long for me to lick off each breast; I felt like a cat some-how. I found I could slurp the sauce from your belly button. And then removing the chocolate from your pubic hair was even more of a thrill for the ears — all sucking sounds, chasing it down to the roots. Past that, there was quiet. I slid my tongue over you, using my fingers to fold back the lips in order to clean the darkness from each crease. And as I continued, all our fluids became chocolate, until I thought it was flowing from you like a fountain.

Come back soon, Nell. I've officially given up sweets until you do.

Max

Monday, September 19, 1983

Dear Nell,

I found your missing sock! Jack had taken it back into the hall closet, under the shelf. I saw him sneak in there with a dishrag last night and decided to go in after him. I don't know what a dog needs with all this stuff, but Jack had squirreled away quite a stash. A veritable Salvation Army store, filled with bits and pieces of used lives. He had the sleeve from one of my old flannel shirts. (I can't for the life of me figure out why there's just the one sleeve.) There were a few of his real toys — chew bones, rubber balls — the sleeve, your sock, a pair of panties I think you lost when you were here in March.

I wonder if Jack wants those things for a reason. Does he like having our things, so that he has US, even when we aren't here? I let him keep the sleeve. You can have the sock when you come down next month, but you'll have to fight me for the panties. I have my own hiding places, my own stash of pilfered totems.

I found your note at breakfast when I went into the pantry for the honey for my English muffin. I should have known you might leave something there. We're such damned slobs, Nell. I had to leave the water running on the honey jar for half an hour to get rid of the playful stickies. A sponge sufficed for the bedposts. The note, on the other hand, was impossible to clean and may be permanently stuck to this desk by the time I'm through. It is, however, legible (and probably edible, depending on one's mood).

So, you've given me an assignment to write about. I haven't had an assignment in years. I wonder if I can stand the pressure. Writer's cramp, headache, dyspepsia… This isn't for a grade, is it?

1. *How did it feel the first time you were in a woman?*
Wonderful. Frightening. I didn't move for what seemed like the longest time. I just stayed there, looking in N.J.'s eyes, feeling her vagina contract around me. She told me later she couldn't help doing that. She said she could feel my pulse beating inside her. And every time her muscles tensed, it was like a series of rings tightening around me, starting at the base of my dick and moving up, slowly. Then I couldn't help but tense up — my dick suddenly pushing upward with nowhere to go. It was too wonderful, really. I came almost as soon as we started to move. After that, we kept still, waiting for my erection to return, but it never did. It was a poor, but predictable, start to one's sex life. But still wonderful. Nothing could have been better than that warm, wet grip she had on me.

2. *What's your favorite part of my body?*
Your legs. More specifically, the backs of your thighs. There's this arc to your thigh when your foot is raised up on something — like when you're drying yourself after a shower and you put your foot on the edge of the tub.

Right then, the back of your thigh describes an arc reminiscent of a French curve. Curves one way. Curves back. I want to draw it, every time I see it. Does it surprise you that I'm so visually inclined? But, Nell, you know I am. You see the way I watch your every move. I memorize the curves. I salt them away like Jack salts away items of clothing. Even now, I can trace that curve in the air with my finger. I own that curve; it's mine.

3. *If you could change your body, what would you do?*
Oh, gosh. Such a thing to ask. I don't care I'm losing my hair, because there's plenty left. I don't want a bigger cock; this one works fine. I'd like my feet to be less ugly, but then, everybody wants that. I want less padding around my middle, but I don't want to give up beer or French fries. But sure. That's it. That's what I'd change: my love handles. I don't want them. You asked.

4. *What's your favorite way we make love?*
What's *your* favorite way? Each time, each way is so different. Even when we do it in the same place and in the same position, it's never the same way twice. However, if I have to choose one thing that stands out — and that does seem to be the purpose of this assignment — then it would be this: My favorite time (not "way," sue me) making love with you was a year ago April. Outside. At night. In the grass. In the rain. The distant lightning made your skin a pale blue. We both sat upright, with you straddling me and my knees pressed against your sides and back. Rocking back and forth, we fucked the storm to sleep. That's my favorite way, Nell. Giving us back to the world.

I know you didn't mean to, but now I'm sitting here, missing you terribly. I've traced the curve of your thigh on the desktop a hundred times now. I walk to the front screen-door, check the mail (which isn't due for several hours), and walk slowly back to my chair. I miss you more than you know. When will you be back, Nell? Do you really exist outside this house, our bed, the Hampton county line? Why don't you want me to ever visit you?

It's clouding up. I hope this finds you well and missing me, too. We'll be here, Jack and I, when you return next month. Until then, Jack has his sleeve, and I have your bikini briefs. He and I will each take what's ours to our secret places and hold them close, remembering, twitching our way into dreamy contentment.

Fondlingly,
Max

Tethered

She couldn't move her arm. Her trusty right hand? Almost useless. The same hand she had used only minutes before to punch a pissant ass pincher. The same hand she had also used to slap a boy dressed as a hot tamale who obviously thought Bourbon Street was crowded enough to get away with fondling her breasts in broad daylight. The ass pincher was apologetic. And the tamale? She left him crumpled inside his foam rubber suit at the corner of Toulouse Street, leaning against a light pole and gasping for air. A good time was had by all.

But now, a block or two closer to Canal Street, the crowd had closed in for real and Maia's arms were pinned to her sides. She could still breathe but, at the same time, Maia felt crushed as if the crowd were a hand whose fingers were closing around her and squeezing hard.

Where the crowd moved, she moved. Up, sideways, forward. Maia found she could pick her feet up off the ground and let herself be carried along by the grip of other shoulders and arms pressed against her. "I am a sardine," she thought. "A sardine in a lame ass costume." She was beginning to regret having those two shots of Jägermeister before getting on the streetcar Uptown.

She was here at Mardi Gras with her housemates, Jason and Terri. Jason wasn't in costume; he wore beads and was trying to carry off that lack of imagination as festive. Terri was dressed as something with leather straps and breastplates reminiscent of Xena, Warrior Princess.

And Maia? Terri had convinced Maia to wear something similar to a toga — basically a cinched sheet that made Maia look like a cross between a pillowcase and a parachute. "Actually, I meant to go as Greek dressing, and this is what Terri thought I meant," she had told Jason. But now, pressed between Jason and Terri, all she really wanted was a pair of shorts and a safety pin.

"Dammit! Whose hand is that?"

She and the others had been carried along by the crowd, moving and turning to find the latest coed baring her breasts for beads on the balconies overhead. Maia had surrendered to the motion of the crowd. She was starting to feel warm and faint from it. Not from the heat of the New Orleans afternoon, but from the crowd itself. Everyone was supercharged and waiting for the next electric spark to jump.

The clamor made Maia's vision hazy, as she watched a blonde on someone's shoulders lifting her shirt and shaking her breasts from side to side in a hail of plastic necklaces. "They want her, but can't have her," Maia thought. It was almost like all of the actual desires were trapped closer to the street surface; there wasn't room for them to bubble up to the level of these yelling faces.

"What the FUCK?" Maia jerked. "But there *is* enough room for some drunken shithead to be sliding a hand up my thigh," Maia thought. She shot Jason a look. The hand was on his side. He smiled and leaned around Maia to whisper something to Terri.

There was a new performer on the balcony across the street. Like a herd of cattle suddenly confronted by a pasture of purple grass, the crowd didn't quite know what to do about the gender-bending redhead. Her hair was feminine, but her face was made up to look masculine. She wore a man's suit pants and jacket over a purple sequined tube top. She leaned over the railing, opened her jacket, and invited the crowd to see her cleavage.

Naturally, some frat boy yelled "Show your tits!" and thought better of it as his friends elbowed him, taunted him. "Dude, that's a guy!" But then someone else said it… "Show your tits!" and then another… and soon it was the same chorus of voices as before, the same bleating herd that had yelled it at the blonde with the 80 strands of beads.

If the girl on the balcony wasn't a stripper, then she was certainly a natural performer. She turned her back to the crowd as she took off the jacket and handed it inside the window to a friend. She turned and strutted back to the balcony rail. Reveling in the transitory adulation, she pulled up her tube top to flash her underboobs. The crowd ate it up. The chant of "Show your tits!" started up again, this time louder.

At first, the girl teased at taking off her top, then pretending to change her mind. But then, she suddenly whipped her top off over her head and started dancing — topless — to the sounds of jazz coming up from the club below. The crowd went wild. Necklaces arced through the air. The girl caught a few strands and put them on. The others fell onto the balcony. "Real or not, those are better breasts than mine," Maia thought.

The hand on Maia's thigh was beneath the sheet, inside her costume, and getting awfully high up her leg. She tried to turn away, but there wasn't any room to either move or turn. She couldn't even move either arm enough to hit or pinch. "It's got to be Jason. Look at him smiling." She tried to stomp his foot, but when she lifted her leg that inch, the hand inside her costume quickly slid between her legs. Her knees buckled, but she was wedged between bodies so tightly that it was impossible for her to fall. She scowled at Jason, but he ignored her.

On the balcony, the topless redhead was slowly unzipping her pants. The crowd didn't seem to know what to expect as she reached inside her pants and unfurled a long, thick cock. The crowd howled. She — or was that he? — held the cock out for everyone to admire. Women down in the street took beads off their own necks and tossed them skyward, trying to snag them on the veiny pink pole.

Maia wanted to give herself permission to just let go, to not feel violated. If the hand was Jason's — or Terri's, for that matter — would that be so awful? It would be something that happened between them, perhaps never even discussed. And if this hand belongs to a stranger in the crowd? Creepy, but... Mardi Gras is a moment. Masks or no masks, the revels of Carnival are primal. It isn't in us to resist today when God isn't expecting us until tomorrow.

The redhead pranced back and forth along the balcony railing, waving the cock to the crowd below. "Told you she was a dude," said one of the frat boys. "Asshole," Maia thought. "She's had you going the whole time." And sure enough, that was the moment the redhead pulled the cock completely out of her pants and held it aloft, revealing that it was silicone all the time. The crowd went wild.

The more Maia wiggled, the more she tried to get the fingers out from between her legs, the more excited she got. The fingers stayed, pressed against her clit, sliding over her vulva through the damp cloth of her underwear. Maia wiggled; the fingers wiggled back. She moved a little to one side with no luck. She tried to move just her hips forward, but there was no room for her hips to go. The fingers followed. The fingers pressed on.

The redhead on the balcony was now performing fellatio on her own fake cock and everyone was watching. Maia was watching, even though she now had strange, uninvited hands stroking and prodding her from both front and rear. A second hand had slid between Maia's legs from the other side. Terri's side. Maybe it was Terri. But Terri wasn't even looking at her. Terri was looking at the redhead, just like everyone else.

Maia closed her eyes. She let the sounds of all the drunks and tourists, the people in masks and face paint, grow quiet in her head. She concentrated on the hands between her legs, the way the fingers moved. It reminded her of when she would masturbate on her stomach, one hand under her, fingering her clit from the front, and the other hand reaching around from behind, fingering her vulva from the top. This was like that. Two hands with one purpose.

The show on the balcony was over. The redhead tossed the dildo into the crowd below, blew kisses left and right, and finally disappeared through the open window to a huge round of applause. The crowd's attention immediately shifted to two young women on the balcony two buildings closer to Conti Street. Their tops were up around their necks. They leaned toward each other and their breasts touched as they started to kiss.

Another hand slipped inside the sleeve of Maia's toga and began playing with her left breast. She was wearing a camisole and the fingers found her nipple already hard and sensitive. Maia looked at Jason again. He smiled and raised his left hand, waving his fingers in her face. The fingers circled her nipple, then squeezed. The two hands between her legs were working back and forth, meeting in the tender middle where her pussy throbbed. That was one of Terri's hands on Maia's shoulder. "Three hands on me, two hands showing," Maia thought. She didn't understand. She stopped trying to understand before a fourth hand slipped inside her other sleeve and cupped her right breast. "I could reach these two hands, if I wanted to," Maia thought. "I could snap a finger." But she didn't try. The crowd was making her feel good.

And then came the beads. Maia couldn't see, but she imagined that they were a set of the fake pearls that used to be so coveted during Mardi Gras before the arrival of the hand-strung globe necklaces and flashing LED beads. These would look like large pearls. Smooth, about an inch in diameter, strung together in a long rope. Pearls with a glandular condition. It wouldn't have surprised Maia if someone had been tossing anal beads. It's New Orleans and it's Mardi Gras. But in her increasingly fuzzy mind, she thought of pearls. There were pearls where she didn't expect pearls. Hard and just as insistent as the fingers.

She was already too weak in the knees to know much more. Mardi Gras. Tomorrow is ashes and no looking back. All Maia knew for sure was that the first hand had pulled her soaked panties to one side and the second hand had just pushed a bead up inside her pussy. She half-heartedly struggled, but the hands on her breasts tightened. Surrender? Another bead, then another.

Submit. Enjoy. Let go.

As the crowd roared at another set of naked tits, Maia felt another bead press upward and pop inside. And that was the end. Maia shuddered and though she willed it to stop, to not come… it came anyway, like Christmas in Whoville. Right there on Bourbon Street, in the bright sunlight, surrounded by thousands of people, Maia had an orgasm. And then… she fainted — suspended there, hung between bodies, resting on the hands of strangers and friends.

Maia came to in the foyer of the Royal Sonesta. She was lying on a couch with a young paramedic hovering overhead. He held her wrist and took her pulse. "He has gorgeous eyes," she thought. "Whoever he is."

Maia tried to sit up, but slumped back down. She looked at the paramedic and asked, "How did I get here? I don't remember…" Her breasts hummed. Her pussy vibrated. She felt the same way she felt having great sex, that anxious period between her first orgasm and her second.

"You fainted, Miss. I think maybe you just got overheated or dehydrated in the crowd. Someone's gone to get you a Gatorade. You should stay right here with me until they get back." He smiled at her.

"Thank you. I don't want to be any more trouble… " It was more of a chaise lounge than a couch. The woman working the hotel Reception desk was giving her a look. "She thinks I drank too much," Maia thought.

"Miss, it's no big deal. It's my job. And believe you me, I've seen lots worse last night and today."

"Still, I feel silly being here in a hotel lobby in this costume." It was true. Maia could see the heads of people in the crowd out the window and could hear the muffled noise. But the doors and windows were closed. And no one inside the Royal Sonesta was wearing a costume except her. She tried to move onto her side and felt something roll across her leg — something inside her costume, something tugging, something hanging. Something still there.

"So, what are you supposed to be, anyway?" the paramedic asked. He was still holding her wrist and she could feel her pulse just as easily as he could.

Maia smiled at him. She didn't tell him that she didn't even care that she had lost count. And she didn't tell him what she was thinking...

"I'm a parachute. I'm a parachute. Pull my cord."

Catching Snowflakes

"Over here! We can be the first ones!"

I watch you walk slowly through the deep snow, lifting and placing your boots to keep from falling. You've started walking up a small, treeless hill and away from the trail we've been following through the woods. In the 24 hours since it snowed, several people and their dogs have been on the trail. But you're right. No one has been up that hill. Not a single footprint can be seen anywhere in front of you. The snow on the hillside is smooth, white, and intact.

You turn and wave, urging me to catch up with you. You're enjoying this. You love winter. Your cheeks and nose are pink, but your eyes are bright blue. You aren't even cold. You wore a skirt! Granted, it's a heavy skirt and you're wearing thick tights beneath it. But it's as if you don't even notice that it's just above freezing in the middle of the afternoon. I'm in a down jacket, wondering why I didn't wear the long underwear. Then again, I'm from south of the Mason-Dixon line, not north of the US-Canadian border like you. When it comes to winter fun, you and I aren't playing the same game, never mind playing in the same league.

I'm only halfway up the hill. You've already reached the top and disappeared. By the time I get to the hilltop, you are part way down the other side. Where are you going? I stop and rest, taking in the view. The forest and the trail are behind me. I'm looking in the other direction, out over snow-covered farms that stretch on for miles, disappearing into the next county. There isn't even a house as far as the eye can see. Just rolling hills and fields, all covered in snow.

Down the hill, you are spinning in circles and laughing. And then, your spinning slows and… plop! You fall over backwards into the fresh snow.

"Come down here and make snow angels with me!"

You move your arms in sweeping arcs, pushing the snow aside to make angel wings. You're very happy. Honestly, I'm cold, but I admit I'm amused to see you out in your element this way. I walk down the hill, following in your footprints, and stand above you, smiling.

"Nice cherub! You've obviously done this before."

"Semi-professional. With the right snow, I can also do a fairly accurate moose."

"Not a beaver?"

"Angels are good for you amateurs. Come on! Fall down! Just one angel!" you say, propped up on your elbows, smiling. "I just want to see if you can do it."

"I'm not spinning." I'm already anticipating the shock of the snow that's certain to get under my scarf and into my shirt collar. If I were a kid, I'd be wearing snow pants.

"OK," you laugh. "You don't have to spin around. Just fall back. Plop. Right here." Your smile is even brighter in the snow.

"This is going to be cold," I think. "I bet people are in short sleeves in New Orleans right now." Backwards I go.

Despite my size and weight, it doesn't hurt to land. Sinking eight or nine inches into the snow has a way of softening the impact — like a pile of leaves without the risk of encountering acorns or sticks.

For a moment, it's almost peaceful, like the moment after a car crash when all you hear is the hubcap rolling down the street. I close my eyes and try to listen to the silence of the hillside. All I really hear is the quiet crunch of the snow on either side of my head, just outside my knit hat. I haven't started feeling chilled yet. There's still time to make some wings and get back on my feet before my pants get wet and the snow in my boots starts to melt.

Or something else might happen.

You throw yourself flat on top of me before I have a chance to either make wings or move out of the way. Short of tossing you off, there's no way I'm getting up. Then again, with your warm lips pressed to mine in a long kiss, I'm less likely to remember that I was even thinking of getting up. Your tongue touches my lips, looking for my tongue. It feels so warm. Our breath forms a little microclimate cloud around our faces as we kiss and kiss and kiss. In a cartoon, this is where we would melt deep into the snow, disappearing from view in a geyser of hissing steam.

Your hands are on my shoulders, your forearms on my chest, supporting half your weight as we kiss. But the rest of you — the part from our chests down — that part of you is moving, pressing, grinding against me. Beneath two thick coats, one pair of pants, one skirt, one pair of inconsequential dinosaur boxers, and a pair of rib knit tights, our bodies react as if this is summer at the beach or autumn in the backseat of a parked car or two teens on the couch in the TV room while the parents are reading upstairs. This is just like dry-humping with extra padding and snow in your hair.

You sit up and rock back on your haunches, smile, and toss your mittens aside. Vive le Quebec! You unzip your coat and I allow you to unzip mine as well. So when you lower yourself onto me again, our coats part to either side, no longer in the way. I feel your body radiating warmth, reflecting warmth back from me as our bodies press together again in the snow. Without those layers of goosedown and Hollofil between us, you quickly find just the right spot in my pants to ride. I raise my head to kiss you harder, seeing the bright white of the snow peeking through the strands of your hair draped around my face.

It has been my experience that women, whether they were riding me from the top or being dry-humped by me from above, have enjoyed frottage more than I have. That is, I feel the grinding, the pressure, the friction, but that's about it. It's enough to get me hard — which benefits her — but not enough to get off. Maybe it's the extra cloth and stuff of zippers. I don't know.

"Take my gloves off," I say. You pull them off, first the left and then the right, and toss them to the side. My hands get slightly sweaty inside gloves, so they start to get cold as soon as the gloves are off. I find the edge of your sweater and quickly slip my hands beneath.

"Better," I think. It's a lovely erection I'm having and my hands have found their way to your breasts (even if they'll never manage to get your two shirts untucked and find bare skin), so this is far from a waste. And you are having such a good time. "Hump away."

But then, you just as quickly change your mind. "Stay there," you say to me, getting to your feet. At first you just stand up where you are, your legs on either side of me and facing the end of me that doesn't have feet. You carefully step to one side, then step back over me, reversing directions. Now you are standing, again straddling me, but facing my feet. You shuffle backwards until your feet are closer to my shoulders and I am looking up your skirt.

I watch you sway your hips from side to side, slowly sliding your skirt up your legs, revealing more and more of your legs in their ribbed knit tights. Slowly, you bend your knees. Your skirt is almost up to your ass as you sway back and forth, getting lower and lower.

Your upside-down head peers at me from between your legs and you laugh "I don't want you to get cold," you say, pulling your skirt out and away from your ass as you completely lower yourself to the ground. And me? My head is *inside* your skirt. Your skirt is a tent and, inside the tent, my face is looking up at the afternoon sunlight filtering through the wool knit cloth and looking at your bottom in tights, near my face. I raise my head enough to kiss you through the cloth. Meanwhile, your hands have unzipped my fly.

At first, I'm not aware of the cold. I feel you lick my cock slowly, several times. Then I feel you grip my cock with just your thumb and forefinger, stroking me, sliding the skin up and down the shaft, but touching me in only those two places. And so the sensation of the strokes masks how the rest of my skin, skin that was just wet from your tongue, is now cooling in the winter air. I feel the cold air more where it seeps into my open fly, sinks around the base of my cock, settles through my hair, and tickles my scrotum, taut and shriveled and no doubt resembling a large walnut.

So, no. I don't feel that my cock is cold, even though I know it must be. I don't quite understand that — how cold my cock is — until a minute later when I feel the warmth of your breath and then the incredible heat of your tongue as you wrap your mouth around the head. Everywhere that isn't touched, every part of me that isn't in your mouth, feels cold. It's so obvious and it had escaped me until just that moment when you suddenly made clear to me what warmth feels like.

You make quick work of me. Once again, you take your mouth away and just use your fingers to stroke me, more quickly now. But this time, I really do feel the cold air on my skin. I imagine the head of my cock growing icy and white. So when you take the head back into your mouth, that's enough to push me over the top. As I gasp out loud, you take me deeper into your mouth and suck me dry, each hot spurt disappearing into a hotter mouth tongue throat. And then, quickly, before it gets cold, you tuck my still wet, fading cock back into my pants and re-zip my fly. My heart is still racing.

Inside the tent of your skirt, my breath and your round bottom have made a toasty nest. It smells of wet wool and wet you. Your pussy is inches from my face. I raise my head just a bit and nuzzle you with my nose. The cloth of the tights is damp. I can feel it, smell it. You don't have anything on under the tights. I can feel how my nose is rubbing, sliding over your vulva, just slightly between your labia. And you feel my nose. You lower yourself, backing up a bit, wanting more.

By touch and by sight, I sort out skirt from tights. I slip my fingers inside the tights waistband and start to pull them back and down over your ass and behind my head. You lean forward a little, which makes it easier, but I need your help to move them far enough down your legs for me to pull both front and back together and get the bunched up cloth under my head, into the snow. Under your skirt, your ass is exposed. Your pussy is exposed. Both of these parts radiate warmth, hovering there above my face as you sit up and arch your back, positioning your pussy maybe an inch above my waiting nose, mouth, and tongue.

At first, I simply graze the insides of your thighs with my cheeks and my afternoon razor stubble. Closer and closer, I slowly lift my face toward you. I touch and then I withdraw. And in this dance, you moan a little and back up, lowering yourself, chasing my face with your fluttering, backlit vulva.

Without touching, my nose hovers an eyelash away from you. I breathe in your smell. Stronger than the winter's brisk snow freshness. Stronger than the wet wool. Stronger than peppermint and pine and gingerbread. The smell of your pussy is stronger than all of those and a hundred times more inviting.

At first, it's just the gentlest nervous touch of my nose on your labia. Nothing more. But then it's a rubbing of your lips along this side of my nose, then a more insistent brushing along the other side, and then a long slow trip down the middle, my nose slipping between your folds, moving clit to hole and back.

I can no longer tell whether I am fucking you with my nose or you are using my nose to get yourself off. Either way, one could safely say you are riding my nose. Your hips are wiggling, your back flexing, your pussy sliding and grinding over the bridge of my nose, nestling the tip of my nose as deep in you as you can before popping up, moving forward, and reloading to slide back again. I nod my head, letting my nose rise to meet you. I breathe through my mouth and my nose when I can.

It isn't so much that I hear your breathing as I feel it transmitted through your thighs into my ears. What I do hear is muted — your moans, the way you say my name. All these sounds are coming to my ears through you, not through air. And they are all arriving in stereo with a background track of blood pumping through your legs.

I grip your hips with my hands and pull you in, planting my nose as deep inside you as I can. At the same time, my tongue finds your clit and begins tracing an infinity sign, circling around, leaving, circling below and then trailing back. You taste like you.

Soon — I think it's soon — you stiffen. You stop moving. I suck your lips, your clit into my mouth, and tongue them with a rapid flick. And with that you're there. I have to hold on tight to stay with you as your climax makes you shudder and rock and cry out. But I do hold on, still licking through the first wave, the second wave, and then a third.

When you stand up — which you can't do at first because my head has your tights pinned to the ground — your skirt lifts away from my face, exposing it to the sun. I close my eyes, preferring the red of my eyelids to the harsh sunlight. I try to ease my eyes open, but the light reflected by the snow is so bright that I'm ready to confess to something even though no one has asked me a thing.

I can make out that you are brushing snow off of your tights, which seem to be soaked through from top to bottom. You pull them up anyway.

"You must be freezing," I say. "How could you kneel in the snow for that long?"

You notice the way I'm blinking and you move to try to get between me and the sun. In shadow, I open my eyes and see that your face is pink. Your eyes sparkle.

"Meh," you shrug. "How could you have your ass in the snow for that long?"

Dammit. Now that you mention it, I'm suddenly aware that my pants are cold and wet from lying in the snow.

"I know a good way to warm us up when we get home," you say, offering me your hand to help pull me up. "Or you can have hot chocolate."

"I think I'd like both." You laugh as I brush the snow from my pants and jacket as best I can.

You turn and start walking back the way we came. This little hill is no longer pristine. But then, I think it may snow again tonight and no one will ever know the difference.

"Come on! Hurry up!" You yell back to me from the top of the hill. "Your legs will freeze! That won't do either of us any good."

No one needs to know. Winter keeps secrets.

Red Ropes

Mmm. I can feel you in my mouth. I love it when you wrap your fingers in my hair and fuck my mouth like this. I love the taste of your skin, the silken hardness of your hot cock filling my mouth and throat. I want to bring you so much pleasure. I want to swallow you and drink every last drop of you while I finger my clit until it hums. I want you to fill me, use me, fuck me. I want… I want…

The sound of your key in the front door shakes me from my fantasy. I open my eyes. You're home!

Before the door opens, I quickly drop to the floor in the front hallway, assuming the position you requested. I kneel, sit on my calves, bend forward with my arms outstretched on the floor. I stare down at the carpet in front of my nose. "No looking up," you said. My panties are there, maybe a foot to the right of my head. I am naked.

I hear you open the door, walk in, close the door, and put your keys in the dish on the table. You aren't surprised to find me this way. It's our playtime and this is what you requested when you texted me from the train 15 minutes ago. All you said was, "Be ready for me when I get home." I am ready. I am so ready for you and for this.

After two years, we're probably still the world's worst at dominance and submission. We choke on the schtick. I can't call you Master or Sir without one of us cracking up. At the same time, we've found that I really enjoy the lighter third of the BDSM spectrum: bondage, discipline, orgasm denial, a little pain. Mostly, what I want is to let go, to relinquish control. And you indulge me. You reluctantly take the reins and you play the part. I trust you in this. If you aren't my Master, you are at least my spirit guide and teacher.

All I see is your shadow moving across the carpet. All I feel is the roughness of the carpet against my hard nipples and my cheek. The roughness is like an exquisite torture on my skin. My skin wants to be touched, but that comes later. I hope it comes later. My nerves are screaming. I want to hold my breath, but my heart is beating too fast. I bend farther down and wait. I wait.

Slowly, your shadow circles me. You walk around me, examining me from every angle. The blood rushes to my face. I am yours now —a sentient fuck toy. My face isn't the only part of me that feels flushed with blood. I could swear that I can smell my own desire.

You stop in front of me. I reach out to kiss your feet, to lick your black leather shoes, but you step back. "No," you say, firmly. "Put your head down until I tell you to move." I instantly retreat. My knees chafe on the rough carpet as I lower myself again, making myself smaller. I'm trembling. Did I displease you? Wasn't that OK?

Then I hear you say, "Show me. Show me that you're ready for me."

So I present myself to you. Gladly, I put more weight on my chest and shoulders so that I can reach my arms back. With my hands, I spread my ass cheeks wide for you. Proudly, I show you my asshole and my pussy. I feel my asshole clench, release. Are you looking? Do you like what you see? My pussy flutters. I know you are able to see how aroused I am. My fingers edge between my legs and spread the lips apart. I can feel that they're thick with blood. I imagine their color as deep pinks and purple brown. Does the light from the window reach this far or is my pussy in shadows? Can you see how wet I am? I moan softly, even though I know I shouldn't. There are rules.

Everything has been discussed and negotiated. We have a safe word, but I've never needed to use it. I trust you. When it's playtime, you have full access to all of me. You know that. I am yours to take and use. I play at being afraid that I will not be good enough for you, that you will find me lacking in some way. Sometimes, I get so lost in the moment that I forget my needs. But you never do.

I know you are looking at me as I kneel here on the floor at your feet, naked and spread wide. No one has ever inspected me like this before. This is my gift for you. I am a gift for you.

You kneel behind me. I arch my back to tip my ass and pussy up toward where your face must be, looking down at me pulling myself apart for your gaze, opening myself for you like the pages of a book. Are you going to look or touch? And if you touch, will it be with tongue, finger, or cock? I bite my lip, waiting.

The answer is finger. You slide one finger inside me, rotate it, wiggle it, then slip it out and back in again. I close my eyes and concentrate on what it feels like as you fuck my pussy with one finger… now, two fingers, sliding in and out as I greedily contract around them. You aren't touching my clit, but… the knuckles! I shudder every time the knuckles pop in or out of me.

If I gave it any thought, I'd be amused that I am happy beyond the act itself. The part that feels good feels really, *really* good. But then there's how content, how *smug* I am just because of the mind-fuckery of the scene. It's not our first time, so maybe I adopt the submissive mindset more quickly or more easily than I did two years ago. But there it is. I'm happy right now in a subbie way. I'm happy to let go and happy to be worthy of your attention. We are both taking. We are both giving.

The texture of your fingers is indescribable. They're so strong and hard, filling me, fucking me, opening me… I gasp slightly as you've added a third finger. Now it's like a cone plunging in and out of me — narrow at your fingertips, flaring wide just inches in, stretching me open. I can hear the slurping sound of your fingers, slick from my juices, thrusting, twisting in and out of me. I can feel the air leaking around the fingers and inside me.

And I can feel my orgasm rushing at me. But you feel it, too. You know my body so well that you know exactly where I am — and you're not ready to give that orgasm to me. I hear you whisper, "Not yet, sweetie. I'm not done with you yet." I am sure that I won't be able to hold back… and I honestly don't want to hold back. But just then, right when I am on the verge of coming, you pull your fingers out of my dripping cunt and get to your feet.

No! I squeal in protest, even though I know you won't approve. I let go of my ass cheeks and throw my arms to the floor in front of me, allowing me to lift my chest and face off the carpet. I feel empty. My ass and pussy are still tipped open and pushing back toward you, needing to feel you inside me again. The air feels cold. My pussy is swollen with blood and yet the skin is so cold on the outside where my juices are evaporating from my lips.

I arch my back, lifting my ass further toward you, toward where I think you are, begging you to finish me.

I think to myself, "Please! Please fuck me! Make me yours! Please, please fuck me!" But I know that I'm not allowed to say this out loud. I can't complain. I can't beg. But I also can't help myself. Softly, I say "Please?" But I'm saying it to no one. You don't hear me. You're no longer here. You've left the hallway entirely.

I hear the sounds of you moving furniture in the living room. The sounds are muffled, almost as if my hearing has given up half its strength to my legs so that they can keep me kneeling here in the hall. It sounds like you are dragging the couch and tables over to the side of the room. I think I hear you picking up and putting down something large — maybe the upholstered chair. I'm not sure. I'm impatient, but I do not move.

Then I hear you walk from the living room to the bedroom. I turn my head in that direction, my cheek pressed to the carpet, so that I can see you when you return. I wait. I imagine you changing clothes, brushing your teeth, filing your nails. I can't imagine what is taking you so long.

I want to touch myself. I need to touch myself, to sink my fingers inside my cunt, twiddle my clit, and finish what you started. But I know I can't. That's not how this is done. It would displease you. In this reality, we have agreed that you can use me for your pleasure and that you will give me pleasure in return. I am yours, freely given. This pussy is yours. That orgasm I almost had? The one receding into the distance? That is yours as well. In this space, I can't do anything for myself unless it will please you. So I kneel here and I wait. But it's so hard to wait, feeling my pussy throb, my nipples tingle as they rub against the carpet. I will not touch myself. I repeat it to myself. I will not. I will not.

It seems like forever before I hear you coming back. I don't look up as you approach, but I can see the bottom parts of you — your strong lower legs sticking out from beneath your blue robe, your bare feet coming toward me. And… Oh, Master! Trailing behind you, are the ends of our red nylon ropes.

You drop the pieces of rope onto the carpet, inches from my face. I love these ropes! I love the feel of them tied around my wrists, my ankles, my breasts. I love the smell of them. I suppose they don't really have a smell. But I imagine all of the things we have done together that those ropes have witnessed, things that those ropes could smell of if memories had smells to give. I love their red color, the visual texture of their intertwining threads and cords. But most of all, I love what they mean to me, to us. You had me buy this rope and bring it home to you. I knelt naked before you that night for the first time, presented you with the rope, made presents to you of the rope and my body, and agreed to be yours completely. You tied me up for the first time that night using these very ropes, ones cut from that first rope I bought us. The red of the ropes on the floor in front of me dazzles my eyes and my pussy flutters. I need you in me. But I need to please you even more.

"Are you ready?" You are standing in front of me now. Your bare feet are just beyond the rope.

"Yes, I am ready," I say into the carpet. I bite my lower lip. I can never tell whether the anticipation of what's to come is the hardest part or the best part. Either way, my heart is beating fast and hard in my chest.

"Then you may stand up."

I start to get up. I am a bit wobbly, but you offer your arm to steady me. As I get to my feet, I glance at your face for just a second — just long enough to see your soft grey eyes and your lips. I quickly look away. Before I look back down the way I should, I see that the center of the living room is empty except for the one large chair.

I stand before you with my legs together, my head down, my hands clenched in loose fists and my wrists pressed together, ready to be tied if that is what you desire. You bend over and pick up the rope.

"Come," you say, taking one of my wrists in your strong grip and leading me into the living room and over to the chair. "Stand here."

You position me facing the back of the chair such that my belly is pressed up against the upholstery. You have tied me to this chair before, but always sitting on it or in front of it. Never in back. I'll have to lean forward, over the back, to get my arms closer to the chair's wooden arms. It's an old chair, but it's solid. Its legs are thick and spread out wide, so it's almost impossible to tip over. And its back is thick and padded. I'm breathing faster just thinking about it. This will be like flying.

You are standing beside me. I see your blue robe out of the corner of my eye. Since I can't look at you, I look down at my hands, which are resting on the top of the chair's back. I want to touch myself. I want to slip one hand between my legs and grab my breast with the other hand. My nipples are as hard as acorns.

You must have noticed the same thing. You lean forward and take the closest acorn nipple between your warm lips. Your tongue flicks at it and I gasp. Your lips release. You back away just a bit and kiss my breast before sucking some skin into your mouth and biting down. My back arches, but I bite my lip and don't make a sound. When you stand up, I see the red mark on my breast where your teeth have been. It stings, but I feel warmth spreading from that spot all over my chest.

Slowly, you pull my hair to one side, exposing my shoulder, my neck, my ear. You lean close to speak. Your voice is like the red ropes. You speak into my ear, soft but serious, loving but stern. "Remember how we play. Do as you are told. Please me and you please yourself." I know what you mean. I understand. "Now, up on your toes and lean forward over the chair."

You step behind me as I stand on my tiptoes. You place your hands on my sides and, with smooth effortless strength, lift me and place me down, folded in a jackknife position over the chair back. My toes don't touch the floor and dangle in the air. For a moment, I teeter. I grab the chair arms with my hands to keep from sliding either forward toward the seat or back off the chair's back.

Moving around to the front of the chair, you line up my left arm with the arm of the chair and lash them together with one of the red ropes. Knot, wind and wrap, knot. My hand is free to grip and flex, but my forearm is bound tightly to the chair arm from my wrist to just short of my elbow. You methodically repeat the process with my other arm. As you work, I see your cock peeking from the gap in your robe. The head is full and purple with blood. I want it in me so badly… in my mouth, my pussy, buried in my ass. I don't care. I need that cock. Your cock.

You walk around behind the chair and again I feel your strong hands gripping my waist. You pull me backwards, sliding me back off the chair a few inches, sliding me back until I can just feel my toes start to touch the floor, but not quite. My weight is partly supported by the chair's back. But now most of my weight is being supported by my arms, tied to the chair. I am hanging from those chair arms, draped over the chair's back like a winter coat. The chair holds. "Good ol' chair," I think, as I grip the carved wooden ends of the chair arms. I'm hovering, suspended… waiting.

"This should work nicely," you say, rubbing your hand up my thigh and across my naked ass. "You really make a nice display. So pretty."

It hadn't even occurred to me until now to orient myself in the room. If you opened the drapes right now, would my bare ass be visible through the window? Could someone see what we are doing? Nice display. It occurs to me that I want to see what this looks like. We should negotiate photos next time. I'd really like to…

Whap! I cry out from the sudden pain of your hand smacking my bare skin. I should focus. Whap! I bite my lip, trying not to cry out this time. Your hand rubs my ass where you've just spanked. The skin feels warm and tingly. Your palm feels smooth.

"Are you still ready for me?" WHAP! Again, you spank me, harder this time. WHAP! WHAP! Each cheek burns and the tingling is making my pussy itch in a way that means I'm swollen and wet.

"Yes, Master! I'm ready!"

"Well, I should be the judge of that, shouldn't I? Let me see how ready you are."

You spread my cheeks apart. I can feel the air on my asshole. I can feel the chill of the air on my labia. I clench, but your hands have no trouble keeping me spread open. All I've succeeded in doing is to wink at you with two surrendered holes. I hold my breath and wait. My ass must be pink and shiny. I wish I could see my ass. I wish I could

107

see me suspended here, bound for you, being fucked by you. You *will* fuck me, won't you? My pussy contracts, hopeful.

Quickly and easily, you slip two fingers into my pussy again. Oh, yes. I'm definitely ready. I clamp down on those fingers as you move them in and out… once, twice, a third time. If you'll leave those fingers right there for just a little longer, if you fuck me with those fingers just a little more, longer than last time… I try to arch my back, wanting to get just the right spot.

Just as my orgasm is hurtling toward me again like an incoming meteor, you remove your fingers. Not again! My pussy gapes, sad and disappointed. I hold it together. I won't whimper. You wipe your fingers on my ass. I feel my juices evaporating on the warm, spanked skin.

You're still behind me. I can feel your hand on my ass. But then you lean around the chair. I can feel your breath on the back of my neck. Your voice is near my ear when you ask, "Are you my fuck slut?"

For a second, I fight to stifle a smile. *Fuck slut.* We discussed this exact term after a play session a month or two ago. Could you ever call me that? Would I be mad at you if you called me that? Could I ever ask you to call me that? Neither of us likes the word "slut." It's not a word either of us would ever use except as a joke. Try as they might, it still hasn't been reclaimed. So we sat there, drinking wine, and you explained how much you didn't want to ever say "fuck slut," even as part of the scene. But in the end, we decided it made us laugh. We decided to use it as a way of checking in. If we could say it, then we could do it. So, sure. Game on.

"Yes! I am your fuck slut!"

"Good girl."

I feel something larger and firmer than a finger press against my pussy, slide briefly between my swollen labia, and then begin to push inside me. It's not your cock, but it's like a cock. A dildo. But which one? We have three. It's not the glass G-spotter. Glass feels different and that one has all those bulges. Maybe it's the small, straight blue jelly one. I'll know soon enough. Deeper and deeper... No, that's *definitely* not the blue one. This is the 8-inch one with the suction cup base and the wicked curve. I fucked this one attached to the refrigerator door one time when you were out of town.

God, it occurs to me that, if you would just thrust it in and out of me a couple of times, I could have a nice, quick orgasm and then we could play whatever it is you have in mind. That's what we should do. I swear, you can trust me. But you aren't sliding the dildo in and out. It simply presses on until I feel the fake balls nestled against my skin. I try to tip my hips to get some action, but you slap my ass hard with your hand. Fine. We'll do it your way.

"Here's the game we're going to play." I can feel you slightly rotating the dildo inside me as you talk. Because of the dildo's curve, I can feel it tracing an arc inside my vagina. I want to move on it. I want you to move it in me. I want... "You are *not* allowed to come. And no matter what I do with you or to you, you must not let this dildo slip out of you. Do you understand?"

"Yes. I understand." I close my eyes and scrunch up my face. Dammit. My pussy immediately contracts on the dildo, holding on for dear life. But then, I second guess myself. What if I hold on too tight and accidentally push it out? In my head, I'm quickly trying to remember which of those Kegel exercises goes bottom to top rather than top to bottom. Then again, I don't want to do too much, be too active. That might make me come... and that would also displease you. Too much, too little...

While I've been busy thinking about the best approach to gripping silicone without seeming to enjoy it, you have walked around to the front of the chair. I lift my head up as much as I can. You're close enough that I can't look up at your face. With my head up as far as I can manage, I can see your legs, your abdomen, and can almost make out your shoulders... but no more.

I watch you undo the tie of your robe, revealing your belly and your cock. I love your cock. It's inches from my face, hard and warm, throbbing with your pulse. It's an average length, thick, well-proportioned. The veins show, but not too much. For me, the best part is that the skin of your cock is so soft, especially the head, making it even more magical to touch, to lick, to suck.

Is that what you want me to do? My neck is already getting tired and I'm thinking that I can't keep my head up much longer. But I can try. This is something I can do. You can give my mouth your cock and I can make you happy. I lick my lips and open wide.

You step forward and lace your fingers in my hair, grab tight, and pull. You slip your other hand beneath my chin, holding my head up. You slip your cock inside my mouth. I close my lips around the shaft, feel the heat of it with my tongue. Mmm. It's everything I fantasized before, everything I already know from the many times I've had you in my mouth before tonight.

You begin to fuck my mouth. The position I'm in and the way I'm tied to the chair, there's no way for me to move on my own. So it's all you. You thrust slowly and deliberately with your hips. I begin to lose myself in the feeling of your cock sliding passed my lips, over my tongue, the head slipping back into my throat. I close my eyes and lose myself in the deep thrusts, the movement of you inside my mouth and my throat, forward and back, spit starting to drip from my mouth and onto the chair. I want to feel your hot cum in my throat. I want...

THUMP!

Oh, no! Dammit! DAMMIT! The dildo! I forgot about it... I didn't hold on... and now it's on the floor near my feet.

You let out a heavy sigh and withdraw your cock from my mouth. You let go of my hair and allow my head to drop limply back down toward the chair seat. I don't want to see the stupid chair seat! I want to see your abdomen, the skin between the flaps of your robe. I want to see the hair around your navel and the line it draws down into the hair that tickles my nose. I want those things filling my eyes again, making my eyes cross as you pull my hair and slip your cock in and out of my mouth. Fuck.

"You were doing so well, too."

And with that, you turn and walk away. You leave the room! Oh, god. You've left the room again. Where did you go? Bedroom? Kitchen? You could be standing in the hallway, just outside the living room, staring at me as I squirm. Come back! I start to cry.

I feel even emptier than before. So empty...

I don't know how long you are gone from the room. But after what seems to me like the longest time, you slowly walk back in. You stand in front of the chair. I don't look up. "I'm disappointed in you." That's all you say. You sit down in the chair with your back pressed against my head. Your hands rest on my hands; your forearms rest on my tightly-bound forearms. Neither of us is comfortable. Neither of us is satisfied.

"Please," I say, "let me try again."

"Hush," you say without turning around. You sit there in your robe, acting disappointed in me. And I hang here, naked, frustrated, and tied to the chair. My pussy is so hungry that it cries, too.

Eventually, you sigh and get up, walk behind the chair, and pick the dildo up off the floor. "We are going to try this again." You reinsert the dildo and I grip it tight. Not again. I won't let it fall out this time. My toes graze the floor and my fingers unclench and grip the chair arm again as you walk back around to the front of the chair. I raise my head again and open my mouth.

Your grip on my hair is even tighter. You've wrapped my long hair around your hand. It hurts, but I don't care. My mouth is full. My pussy is full. Your cock has lost some of its hardness, but that quickly returns as it moves in and out of my mouth. The rhythm of your pumping away is soothing. I think of the dildo, waving behind me like a conductor's baton. I close my eyes.

I'm surrendering. I no longer even try to keep my head up. I let my neck muscles go and let you have my head to use as you wish. Keep my lips over my teeth. Keep the dildo inside me. And remember to breathe. Those are the three things on my short list of conscious things I need to do. And when that gets to be too much, I can stop breathing.

Faster and faster, you fuck my face, filling my mouth and throat with hot smooth skin. And then…you pause… and I know! I try to look up at you so that I can watch you come. The first hot spurt hits the back of my throat and you moan with contentment. Another and another. I am yours and I did this. Pick a word. I'm your slut, your slave. I swallow, but more fills my mouth. You pull out and the last bit slops onto my upper lip. I lick it off, happy... but not showing it. Not yet.

You unwrap your fingers from my hair and gently let my head down. Finally, I can relax my neck. I leave my mouth open, using it to breathe. Your hand trails over my back as you slowly walk behind me, behind the chair. The dildo is still in me. Hidden beneath my hair, you can't see me smile. Success!

"That was very good, sweetie. I am pleased." Your voice is gentler, your touch on my back and sides kinder. You *are* pleased. I taste of you, smell of you... and you are happy with me. I am happy with me. "It was so good, in fact," you say, running your hands down my back and my ass, "that I am giving you permission to come. Would you like to come now?"

"Yes, please. I would very much like to come." I don't even have the strength to wiggle my ass from side-to-side. So, yes. Please.

In a movie, it would take longer. In a movie, I'd pant and moan and you might change positions several times. But that's not how this is. That's not reality. This is. As soon as you begin to thrust the dildo in and out of me — tens strokes, tops — I come. I come and come and come... over and over and over, like having all of the abandoned orgasms returning home to Capistrano. And for a while, you continue. In and out, in and out. I'm tied to the ground with red ropes, but I'm flying from you and flying back to you, as always... yours.

Daisy Chain

"Holy shit! Do you see *that*?"

"What? Where?"

I start to look around — up the path and between the trees — but no sooner are the words out of my mouth than you shush me, grab me by the arm, and pull me behind the nearest tree trunk. I stumble over a root but manage to grab onto your shoulder to right myself.

It's a lazy, summer morning in the park and no one seems to be around. The rain this morning has made everything smell like wet leaves and potting soil. I notice that there's a leaf stuck to the top of my sneaker and an earthworm just inches to the right, presumably grateful that neither of us has squished it flat.

I know that look on your face. I love it when your eyes get big like this, even though it sometimes means we're about to get into some trouble (e.g., unwise spending, the eating of desserts larger than possums, activities not entirely legal, and so on). What did you see?

You have your index finger pressed to your lips to tell me to be quiet. I don't understand, so you silently, excitedly motion with your other hand for me to peek around the tree to see what's happening in the clearing on the other side. When I look, I see a dark green Army blanket spread out under a tree. And on that blanket, pink and disheveled, I see the two young lovers.

"You have any quarters?"

We had just paid our check and were about to leave the diner, where we had eaten breakfast. I had coffee and challah French toast. You had juice and half a cantaloupe. We had sat there for over an hour, alternately discussing recent Supreme Court decisions, hot sauces, the cult of Arnold Ziffel, our neighbors, Swing music, and finally how much to tip.

You held out your hand as I reached into my pocket and checked my change. "How many do you need?" I could see that you were eyeing the vending machines.

"Two, I think."

I handed you two quarters. "Needing a pocketful of breath mints?"

"Nope. Something else." You checked out the selection and smiled. "See, when I was a girl," you explained, "I would have gone straight for this machine that gives you handfuls of the SweeTart-like candy. Or maybe that one with the hi-bounce balls. But that was then."

You smiled, turned to the last machine, inserted my quarters, and turned the handle. The machine popped out a plastic egg, which you quickly busted open, revealing a plastic "fashion ring" with a fake diamond the size of a globe grape. You quickly put it on your finger and held it out for me to admire.

"See? Sooo sophisticated. Now I'm fashionable and you can take me literally anywhere."

"Literally?" I laughed. You skipped ahead of me and twirled on the sidewalk.

"Yes. Anywhere. Even underwater. Fish love baubles. Or you could just take me to the park. I'll let you shine my rock at some ducks!"

The man on the blanket is older than we are, maybe closer to 30 than early 20s. His jaw is large and his chin is square, but otherwise his appearance is unremarkable: brown hair, average build, no distinguishing characteristics that I can see. And I can see quite a bit since his shirt is unbuttoned and his pants and underwear are pulled down past his knees. His cock seems both happy and happily normal sized in the woman's hand. (Note: Porn is nice, but I can see where it might be beneficial to my self-worth to occasionally see an average-sized erection other than my own.)

The woman is a bit younger. She is wearing a burgundy print cotton dress, simple in style, unbuttoned down the front to her waist. Her hair is short and dark and she has tattoos on her arms and one ankle. She is not wearing a bra and I can see the man's hand holding one breast as she sits next to him, slowly stroking his cock. Her panties are balled up near an empty wine bottle. When she kneels between his legs and bends forward, we can see the white roundness of her rear just touching a shaft of sunlight.

You take my hand in your hand. Your hand is warm and a little damp. And your grip is tight as if to say, "We're staying." I nod OK.

Slowly, the woman takes the man's entire length into her mouth and then pulls back, letting it slide out between the tight circle of her lips. She grasps the base with one hand. Now she is using her tongue, just licking the head and circling around the rim. And then back in it goes. Out, then in again, on and on. When I am sure he is about to come, she stops. She leans forward and runs her hands up the taut, smooth skin of his belly and chest. She teases him, hovering her head over his head, letting her hair fall into his face. Then back, back she slides along him... her hands traveling back down his chest, his ribs, his belly.

I suspect you realize how uncomfortable this situation is making me. You know I'm a color-inside-the-lines kind of guy. You don't hold it against me any more than I hold your "fools rush in" exploits against you. This *laissez–faire* attitude about each other's foundational motivations is the basis of our relationship — along with frequent desserts and occasional butt sex.

It's not that you don't care that I might be squeamish or nervous being here, watching these two people have sex. For you, it's situational ethics. You see it as your job to either humor me or push my buttons as needed. I'm always free to say "no" if or when you start getting us — or me — into trouble. This feels like one of those times I'll be fine right up until the moment we're being issued citations or I'm being punched in the nose.

Once more, she takes his cock into her mouth. We can tell that she means business this time. She alternates six or seven head bobs with a dozen strokes with her hands. I imagine that his cock cools outside of her mouth, the air evaporating her saliva from his pink and purple skin. But then she sucks him inside again, heats him up, gets his cock wet again.

Your hand grips my hand more tightly as we both see his body grow rigid. We both can tell. Any minute, any second... There! His upper body jerks and jerks as she first sucks, then licks at him. Then slower, slower...

I can't believe we're watching this. I can't believe we're getting all worked up because we're watching this. I can't believe we're getting all worked up because we're watching this and we happen to be out in the middle of a municipal park where people really shouldn't be doing what these two people are doing and we shouldn't be watching them do it. On the other hand, I want you so much right now that I won't hear the police horse patrol until it's breathing oats down our sweaty, rubber necks. Life's short.

I move to stand behind you, continuing to watch the lovers over your shoulder. You feel the hard bulge in my pants and push back into it, squirming a little from side to side. I put my arms around you and cup your tits in my hands. The rib-knit fabric of your tank top is thin and I can feel your nipples harden immediately between my fingers. You hold my left hand to your breast with your left hand. You reach your right hand behind you and start rubbing the crotch of my jeans. The bulge isn't getting any less hard with the added attention. Neither are your nipples. Still, no matter what our hands may be doing, our eyes aren't leaving the young couple.

They are changing positions, so we pull back behind our tree, hiding a little more until they settle back. Not that they ever seem to look around. Unlike me, they aren't worried about being seen. The woman is now on her back and the man is now kneeling between her spread legs. The bottom of her dress is gathered up around her hips and her knees are up. His hand is under the fabric. I can see it moving and can only imagine what his fingers — no, his thumb — what his thumb is doing there.

The woman's eyes are closed now. She spreads her knees farther apart and inches her skirt up onto her belly.

Her leg blocks my view of his hand. I imagine his hand between her legs, opening her up, separating her folds with his fingers, distributing the nectar and setting the table for his feast. I should've finished my French toast.

Then he crouches down to plant the first kiss on the soft inside skin of her right thigh. His forehead pushes back the fabric of her dress, exposing her wet pubes and labia to the sun and to the air and to our wide eyes. And when his tongue extends and touches her just there in the heart of the wetness, her head rolls back. I pull you closer to me and hear both our breaths catch.

I'm thinking how quiet this all is. From where we stand, we can't hear a sound that the two of them must be making. I know in my head the familiar sounds of my tongue licking you — the sticky clicks, the tiny sucking pops and slurps — but can't hear a thing from them.

Instead, I hear indistinct but familiar city sounds in the distance. Closer to us, I hear birds singing and the wind blowing the leaves over our heads. And as we watch him grab both her thighs with his hands and bury his face deeper into her, I think I hear a bicycle bell on the other side of the park.

Ding, ding.

She brushes the back of her hand across her face, momentarily shielding her eyes from the sun. That same hand then traces the side of her face, her own neck, past her collar bones, and into the open front of her dress.

Ding, ding.

Her head slowly twists sideways. I can see that she's biting her lip, perhaps trying to stifle a cry. Her head tips backwards as her back arches and lifts off the blanket. She's like the mainspring of an old wind-up alarm clock. All that potential energy, stored up and ready to pop.

Ding, ding, ding, ding!

Her back abruptly slams down against the blanket as she collapses forward, grabbing his head with her hands, her fingers in his hair, rocking his head between her legs as she moves from side to side.

The waist of your cargo shorts is loose enough for me to get my hand down into them at the small of your back. The curve of my fingers and palm follows the curve of your bare cheek and I slip my hand inside both your shorts and your panties. Your skin seems to fit my hand, soft and surprisingly cool to my touch. I flex my fingers and rub your ass the smallest amount. I can't reach farther; the waistband has tightened on my arm above my wrist. I look down at the freckles on your shoulder, the way your hair falls around your neck. It's not enough.

I know your cargo shorts have a simple drawstring tie in the front. I reach my other hand around your waist and pull the bow undone. Your shorts loosen and I remove my hand from the rear. Then I quickly squat behind you, pulling your shorts and panties down past your knees.

You stand there, hiding behind the tree, your bare skin and goosebumps shimmying in the late morning air. But you don't even turn around. Your hands are holding onto the tree. Your head still faces forward as you continue to watch what is happening in the clearing. You never turn around. I could stand back and take a picture. I could find someone on the path and invite them to come see. Instead, I quickly stand back up and cover you from behind with my body, resting my chest against your shoulders so you know I'm there.

You move your feet apart, rise up on your toes, and lean into the tree as I slip my hand between your legs from the rear, a few inches below where you want my hand to be. I can tell where my hand is without looking. There's the soft, familiar coolness of your upper thighs. A little higher and there's the smooth, warmer spots near the top where your legs meet. Another half inch and the first touch of hair. Suddenly, there's the wet. Found it. A person might suspect you impatiently bent your knees.

You grip the tree tighter as I press into you. My left hand holds your left hand, clutched, both pressing into the dark, rough bark. My right hand is buried between your legs, the fingers diving into the slippery slick, moving from back to front and back again.

I look over your shoulder, past the tree to the clearing. I know you're still watching as the man slides up over the woman and kisses her. He is balanced on one arm. His other hand is on her bare breast, caressing round and round, under, and then squeezing. Behind the tree, your hips are moving rhythmically back and forth with the motion of my fingers, sliding your hard nub into my fingertips. The man moves his hand from the woman's breast to the side of her hip and arches up and forward.

For the first time, I hear what passes as a sound coming from them — both of them inhaling sharply as he enters her, first a little, and then quickly all the way in. He moves lazily, methodically dipping in and out of her at first, less thrusting into her than undulating over her. The woman's eyes are fully open and she's looking up, but I can't tell from this angle whether she is looking up at his face or past him at the shards of sunlight and the bits of blue sky breaking through the leaves above their heads.

All of the fingers on my hand are wet now and I can feel liquid starting to drip down toward my palm. I dip my middle finger fully into you, straight up at first, then arching back so that it pushes against the front wall of your vagina. I hold it there for a second, feeling you squeeze around my finger, wondering whether you thought to do it or whether your pussy did it all on its own. I pull the finger out, quickly circle your clit with the pad of my sopping fingertip, and then slip back inside you again. I kiss the side of your neck and taste just the slightest hint of salty sweat.

I can tell you are trying hard not to make a sound. I sympathize, but I'm guessing you don't want me to stop. Still, you manage to stifle all but the tiniest of whimpers. Funny, I know that there are birds chirping and somewhere beyond that the sounds of car horns and sirens, but all I can hear right now are your tiny cries, the sounds of my fingers in your dripping folds, and what I imagine as the heavy breathing of the couple we're watching. The world has shrunk to the thrashings of four bodies in a public space.

The couple's subtlety is gone now. The man is moving faster and thrusting harder. The woman's hands are on his sides, holding tight. And whether it's on purpose or not, the pace of how your hips are moving on my hand has started to exactly match the couple's pace — your back and forth dance with my fingers matching the man's push and pull in and out of his lover.

The woman has pulled her legs up and back. Her hands are on her legs now, just below her bent knees. She spreads her legs wide and pulls her knees back toward her shoulders. Faster and harder. Your left hand clutches mine so tight against the tree that your knuckles are white on white, as white as the fake diamond in your vending machine ring. Faster, faster…

And there's a nanosecond in which I know that it's about to happen… and then it does. As the man and woman on the green blanket in the park clearing groan and shake together, you come too. Your knees give a little and your body shakes. You cover your mouth by clamping it down onto your forearm. Your breath is coming fast and deep through your nose. As it passes, you move more slowly on my fingers ... and finally you let go of my bloodless left hand.

You turn around and kiss me. Your eyes are wide and moist. I smile and touch your cheek. "They're leaving," I say, looking past your flushed face for a second to where the couple is quickly dressing.

I hear you unzipping my pants before I can feel it, and feel it before I can see what you're doing, your hair blocking my view of what your hands are doing. The tugging of the zipper, fingers opening the fly, your hand inside my boxers, pulling and tugging until ... I feel air. I'm so hard and excited that my freed cock bobs in the air, up and down with the beat of my heart. You undo my belt and pants and carefully pull everything past my erection so that it all falls to my feet.

Then you turn back around, away from me and back toward our tree, pushing your cool white rear into me. I take my cock in my hand and nestle it between your legs. It touches hair. It touches wet.

You bend over slightly and use one of your hands to guide me into you. And when I push forward, there's no resistance. We're both just that ready. I grab your waist and pull us together, going deeper and deeper inside you. I can feel the wet warmth close in around me in little grips and grabs that maybe you can't even control.

The couple has finished dressing and is gathering up the wine bottle and the remains of their picnic. They look almost normal now. But I've seen beneath that burgundy dress. I've seen the looks on their faces when they come. There's normal and then there's awkwardly familiar.

You are moving your hips as I move in and out of you. One of your hands is flat on the tree trunk, steadying you. Your other hand is between your legs, first rolling my balls, and then jiggling your clit, pushing it down and back into my cock as it moves in and out, forward and back.

Even now, I am aware of what the couple is doing. They are folding their blanket. There's no reason to look their way anymore. Maybe it's habit. Maybe I'm worried that they'll come this way.

I feel the first hint that I'm going to come soon — a little empty feeling deep below the base of my cock. Somewhere, something is moving. You seem to know it, too. You change the pace of your movements and stand up a little more to increase the tightness. I exhale and let go of the need to get somewhere. I'm already here.

And as the couple turns and starts to walk away, I come. I ram as deep into you as I can, my legs starting to turn to willow, to jello. And then you come, too. Neither of us can control the spasms, our breathing. We clutch at each other and the tree just to keep from falling down.

They're gone.

"Well, that was interesting," I say, giving you a quick kiss. The city sounds have returned — traffic, sirens, people everywhere. The clock has restarted.

We both bend over to pick our pants up off the ground. You blot between your legs with your panties, wad them up, and stick them into your shorts pocket before putting your shorts back on.

"I should rinse those out a little before we get on the train," you say, smiling. "I'm drenched." We were planning on catching the subway to Brooklyn to meet friends. "I wonder how long it would take to dry them with one of those bathroom hand blowers."

"I'm trying to picture how that will look."

"Me, too." You laugh. We start to walk away, holding hands. "Wait," you say, turning back. "I think I dropped my phone."

And as I watch you trotting back over to the tree to retrieve your phone, I see a flash of color in the green bushes just beyond. A branch snaps back and leaves rustle. And I think… I think I hear a voice saying, "Shhh."

"What are you looking at?" you ask as you walk back to where I'm waiting.

"I'll tell you later." I smile and take your hand again. "Let's go."

About the Writer

S.A. Harper hails from somewhere south of the Mason-Dixon line and currently lives somewhere unfortunately too far north for a decent oyster po' boy.

Harper's first erotic story was written in middle school. It involved a distracted and inattentive graduate student, several maraschino cherries missing from their jar, and a telltale trail of sticky pink running down a lover's pale white thigh.

There is a slight possibility that Harper isn't so much an erotic writer as a writer in need of a hearty snack.

For other work by S.A. Harper,
please visit:

Word Oyster Press
wordoyster.com

You may contact the writer at:
saharper@wordoyster.com